DEATH AT THE VILLAGE CHESS CLUB

DEBBIE YOUNG

Boldwood

First published in Great Britain in 2025 by Boldwood Books Ltd.

Copyright © Debbie Young, 2025

Cover Design by Lizzie Gardiner

Cover Images: Shutterstock and AdobeStock

The moral right of Debbie Young to be identified as the author of this work has been asserted in accordance with the Copyright, Designs and Patents Act 1988.

Every effort has been made to obtain the necessary permissions with reference to copyright material, both illustrative and quoted. We apologise for any omissions in this respect and will be pleased to make the appropriate acknowledgements in any future edition.

A CIP catalogue record for this book is available from the British Library.

Paperback ISBN 978-1-83518-562-9

Large Print ISBN 978-1-83518-563-6

Hardback ISBN 978-1-83518-561-2

Ebook ISBN 978-1-83518-564-3

Kindle ISBN 978-1-83518-565-0

Audio CD ISBN 978-1-83518-556-8

MP3 CD ISBN 978-1-83518-557-5

Digital audio download ISBN 978-1-83518-560-5

This book is printed on certified sustainable paper. Boldwood Books is dedicated to putting sustainability at the heart of our business. For more information please visit https://www.boldwoodbooks.com/about-us/sustainability/

Boldwood Books Ltd, 23 Bowerdean Street, London, SW6 3TN

www.boldwoodbooks.com

To Pauline and Colin Dixon

PROLOGUE

Who knew that chess could be such a dangerous game? Or is that only in the Cotswold village of Little Pride, which I've recently made my new home? Surely never in its fifteen-hundred-year history has this dignified, sedate game caused as much mayhem as when I introduced it to the village schoolchildren.

My well-intentioned scheme drew a flurry of visitors from beyond the parish, one of them destined to make an onward journey only as far as the local mortuary.

Not to mention the attacks on my little shop – Alice's Cotswold Curiosity Shop, as I'd now renamed it – and on my person.

Even though the whole affair was triggered by an odd request out of the blue from my ex-boyfriend Steven, supposedly heading for India on his motorbike to resolve his midlife crisis, I couldn't help feeling the crisis was of my creation. So what could I do but try to track down the murderer before they could strike again?

With a little help from friends, old and new, and even from my estranged mum, I was determined to give it my best shot. Never before have I so wanted to call checkmate – on the villain whose reckless actions were threatening my village community, my shop and even my survival.

1

OPENING MOVE

'What do you mean, you've spent all your money already?'

It was early September, and Steven, my ex, had only been gone a few months. His motorbike trip to India was supposed to be the start of a new life as a nomad, ending our twenty-five-year relationship. He'd vowed to lead a minimalist lifestyle in future, leaving his accumulated clutter in storage.

'I thought you were going to be living on a shoestring. What's happened? Did you tire of your bargain-basement lifestyle and take to staying in posh hotels along the way?' Steven had never been keen on expensive resorts, so it made no sense that he'd start now. 'Or has your motorbike been stolen?' In which case, insurance would cover it. 'You did take out a global insurance policy, didn't you?'

Steven's lack of attention to detail had caused the huge mess he'd made of the conveyancing for my new home, Nell Little's Cotswold Curiosity Shop. Nell Little having retired to a care home at nearby Wendlebury Barrow, I intended to convert the shop into a home. I discovered only after I'd bought it that planning regulations obliged me to keep open the ramshackle bric-a-brac shop. So, it wouldn't have surprised me to discover Steven had failed to properly insure his precious motorbike before he left. God forbid he'd had an accident, making him liable for huge damages. I couldn't think how else he'd managed to run out of cash so quickly.

'My motorbike is fine, thank you very much,' he replied tersely.

After living with him for a quarter of a century, I could tell he was hiding something.

'It's only a temporary cash-flow issue,' he continued. 'I just need a few grand to tide me over until the next payout from my annuity.'

While I had invested my half of the proceeds from our house sale in my new home, Steven, after lodging enough in a current account to pay his way to India, had spent the rest on an annuity that paid him a regular monthly income.

I closed my eyes, the better to hear the accordion music playing in the background.

'So have you actually reached India yet?'

The music didn't sound very Indian.

The line went silent for a moment, before the accordionist struck up the unmistakeable melody of '*Non, je ne regrette rien*' in the background. Then a third voice piped up.

'Oh, Stevie!' It was a woman's voice, unmistakeably American.

Steven has always hated being called any diminutive of Steven, just as I insist on my name, Alice, always being used in full. Please don't call me Al.

Instantly, I heard Steven clap his hand over the mouthpiece of the phone too late for me not to hear him say, 'Just a moment, darling,' before returning his attention to me.

'Actually, I'm still only in France,' he said at last. 'South of France, to be precise, Nice.'

'Nice?' I echoed in disbelief. 'That's hardly on the way to India.'

Steven coughed. 'No, well, once I'd crossed the English Channel, I decided I might as well take the scenic route and see more of Europe on my way. After all, I don't know when I'll be back this way again.'

I passed my free hand over my eyes. 'So now, don't tell me: you've discovered you can't live as cheaply on the French Riviera as you can backpacking in India. *Quelle surprise.*'

Steven gave a feeble laugh at my schoolgirl French.

'Tell me something I don't know,' he replied. 'Although to be honest, I did think I'd have more than enough after my little flutter in the casino on my first night here.'

'You've been playing cards for money?' Although he couldn't see me, I shook my head in horrified admonition.

'Actually, it wasn't cards, it was roulette. I mean, you can't come to Nice and not have a spin on the tables, can you?'

'That's like saying you can't visit Beachy Head without jumping off.' This extreme analogy was in dubious taste, but I wanted to impress upon him the dangers of his attitude.

'Oh, for goodness' sake, Alice, don't be such a wet blanket. I'm having a fabulous time. This is just a cash-flow problem – a temporary hitch. Besides, I'm not about to ask you to bail me out, if that's what you're thinking.'

He needn't have worried. Just after he'd left, I'd harboured such a hope, but now his comment made me realise that now the notion of him returning to me filled me with horror. I was rather enjoying the new life I'd made for myself here in Little Pride.

'So why are you telling me this?' I asked, thinking, *It is only a day's drive from Nice. He could be home with me in no time if he were really desperate. Please, no!*

His voice brightened. Perhaps he felt he was moving onto safer ground. 'Actually, I was just going to ask you to liquidate some of my assets and wire me the resulting cash to tide me over.'

'How can I do that? Your annuity's cast in concrete, isn't it? You can't undo it. That's the whole point of it – it guarantees a fixed income.'

Unless he found some kind of work, the annuity was his only source of income until his paid employment and state pensions kicked in when he turned sixty-six – another sixteen years away.

'No, silly, I mean by selling some of my collections.' How dare he call me silly, after his confession of financial incompetence? Never mind the mismanagement of my conveyancing. 'After putting some distance between me and them, I realised I'm not so fond of them as I thought. I've had my pleasure from owning them. Now it's someone else's turn. I've realised I've only been their temporary curator, looking after them for future generations. Under the current circumstances, it makes sense to dispose – at a profit – of any items that no longer spark joy.'

Spark joy? Since when had Steven joined Marie Kondo's fan club?

The woman with the American accent had begun to sing in bad and error-strewn French, although to be fair, she was a note-perfect match to the accordion. Was she the Marie Kondo fan? Or was she trying to milk Steven's assets for her own purposes? Perhaps she was some kind of card shark, winning huge amounts of money from him that he had no other way to pay.

Steven, waiting for me to speak, became plaintive. 'I thought you'd be more supportive, but I suppose you never liked my stuff.'

This wasn't entirely true. I had admired some of his collections as works of art or as interesting pieces of history, including, ironically, his numerous packs of decorative playing cards. I just didn't appreciate them constantly scattered about what would otherwise have been a tidy and tastefully decorated house.

But we'd had that discussion too many times. I wasn't about to resume the argument now.

'So, what exactly is it that you'd like me to sell for you?'

I heard the winner's smile in his voice. 'I thought the chess sets would be a good start. There are about twenty of them, and they've got to be worth at least a hundred quid each – the sets, I mean, not the pieces, ha ha.'

If his pause was for me to join in his laughter, he must have been disappointed.

'They should be easy enough to dispose of,' he went on. 'They're all together in the same storage crate, and in each set, you'll find the receipt for what I paid for it and where I bought it. For the more expensive ones, there's also a paper trail proving their provenance, listing previous owners and sales.'

'But I know nothing about chess,' I protested. 'How am I to know what to do with them?'

'Oh, for goodness' sake, Alice, this is the twenty-first century. Just stick them all on eBay. Loads of collectors are constantly watching eBay for collectible chess sets. That's where I bought most of them myself. Easy-peasy.' He chuckled. 'What a shame you didn't keep that little shop open in your new house, eh? My chess sets would look eye-catching in an old-fashioned shop window. Not that anyone worthwhile would have spotted it there. Far better to sell them online.'

I hesitated. Having had no contact from Steven since he'd left the country, he wouldn't have known that thanks to his ineptitude, I'd had to keep Nell Little's Cotswold Curiosity Shop open, and I had now, with her blessing, made my own mark on the place. Nor had I told him I'd lost my job at the museum just before moving in. But I wasn't about to tell him now. I didn't want to make his request seem any easier.

Nor did I want him to know that I was turning the old shop into a viable business, with the support of the local community and the retired owner, Nell Little, who was fast becoming a friend and mentor.

'OK, I'll do it,' I said, realising that helping Steven might also help my shop. Besides, I didn't want to contemplate the alternative – that otherwise, he might have to come back to sell them himself and cadge accommodation from me while he did so. 'That is, if you give me free rein to sell them however I wish, and for any price I think fit. Which will of course be the best price I can get for them. Don't worry, I'm not going to give them away for pennies just to be shot of them.'

It was an offer he couldn't refuse. Besides, I was still on his side really. A quarter of a century of looking out for each other is a habit not easily snuffed out.

'Thanks so much, Alice, I really appreciate your help. And of course, you must take commission for your trouble. 10 per cent OK?'

'Twenty,' I said, biting my lip at my boldness, but I was on my own side too.

'Done.' When he didn't try to haggle, I realised what dire

financial straits he must be in. 'Just wire me what you can, when you can,' he said. 'No need to wait until you've sold every last set.'

I almost felt sorry for his desperate state, until his American lady-friend called, 'Come on, Stevie,' in the background, and I said a hasty goodbye. I'd heard more than enough.

2

AN ADVANCE DEFLECTED

I'd only just ended the call when, through the open back door, I heard the shop door open and a familiar male voice cry out, 'Good afternoon, Alice!'

I returned to the house from my back garden – the only place on my property that I could get a decent mobile phone signal – and hurried through the kitchen and dining room to the shop. Robert, locally nicknamed Bob Sponge for his self-made fortune as the inventor of the everlasting washing-up sponge, was standing at the trade counter, beaming, and clutching in one hand a large bunch of perfect apricot roses.

'Good evening, Robert.' Such was the contrast between my chivalrous next-door neighbour and my self-serving ex that I gave Robert a warmer smile than perhaps he'd expected.

The fragrance of the beautiful roses from his garden was already filling the shop. The widowed Robert, aged about sixty and therefore a decade older than me, had been the perfect gentleman to me since I'd moved to Little Pride. I didn't dare presume his feelings towards me were any more than neighbourly, but as he set the bunch of flowers on the counter, my hopes soared.

Then the shop door flew open again, this time to admit Danny, my former museum colleague and now my lodger.

A few weeks earlier, we'd realised his ex-partner, Martin, out of jealousy had spiked my drink at the pub on the day I was made redundant. It was clearly untenable for Danny to remain living in Martin's flat, so I'd offered him temporary refuge in my spare room until he could find new accommodation on his own. Although I had been content to live alone, after the awful murder of a local builder that took place in the summer, I was glad to have his company, especially as autumn was approaching and the nights were growing longer and darker.

'Hi, Robert, hi, Alice,' said Danny. He strode across the shop floor and lifted the flap in the counter to join me behind it. 'Successful day's trading, I hope?'

I smiled proudly. 'Actually, yes. I sold that little oak writing desk and chair for a decent sum to a passing tourist. Good thing they were driving a big enough car to take it away with them.' I pointed to the gap left by the bureau. 'There it is, gone.'

'Well done,' said Danny.

He'd always been supportive of my new venture.

'Fancy a pint at The Quarrymen's Arms to celebrate? It's a lovely evening, and we should make the most of it while it lasts.' Being teetotal didn't stop Danny enjoying pubs.

To my disappointment, Robert picked up the bouquet again and clutched it to his chest.

'You're welcome to join us if you like, Robert,' I ventured, hoping Danny wouldn't mind.

'No, no, thanks all the same,' replied Robert. 'I only called in to tell you I was planning to visit Nell Little this evening in the care home at Wendlebury Barrow. I'm going to update her on the progress about the paddock next door, now that Terence Bolt has cancelled his plans to build houses there.'

'I'm sure she'll be very pleased to hear that,' I replied sincerely. I knew how upset she had been at that prospect. 'She'll love the flowers from your garden. Do give her my very best wishes.'

He glanced at the tangerine blooms and gave a rueful smile. Perhaps he missed her more than I'd realised. Nell had been a good friend to his mother and a significant person in his childhood.

'Yes, Nell always liked my roses,' he said.

After Robert had gone, I rearranged the shop floor display to fill the gap where the desk had been. Danny leaned on the counter, watching me put the finishing touches to my arrangement.

'I'm sorry, Alice, did I interrupt something just now?' Danny asked gently. 'Between you and Robert, I mean?'

I shook my head without turning round to face him. How could I assume a debonair magnate of industry like Robert might be romantically interested in an amateur, hand-to-mouth shopkeeper like me?

'No, of course not, he was just being neighbourly,' I asserted, as much to persuade myself as to convince Danny. 'He knows I like Nell. I might pop over to see her again myself soon. Anyway, I've got far juicier news for you. I got a call from Steven today. He wants me to sell some of his collections, starting with the chess sets. He needs the cash, you see. I know nothing about chess, but I could hardly say no without sounding petty, could I? I'm trying to be the bigger person here.'

Danny's eyebrows shot up in surprise. 'Really? That's a bit of a cheek, leaving you to do the work while he's off having fun. But don't worry. I'll help you flog them. I know a lot about chess sets. I've always enjoyed playing chess. Now, let's rustle up a quick dinner, then you can tell me all about it while we eat.'

'Actually, before we do that, would you mind coming with me to the twenty-four-hour self-storage warehouse to collect the chess sets? It's halfway between the Broadwick and Little Pride, so not a long journey. I'm anxious to get going on Steven's project as soon as possible. He sounded a bit desperate for money. But I don't fancy going there by myself. Those places always look a bit creepy.'

That was an understatement. The high-security building, with tiny windows like arrow slits dotted around its steel-grey, concrete walls, struck me as positively sinister. I'd driven past it a number of times, but never seen a living soul there, although I presumed there must be at least one security guard lurking in the shadows. I'd have felt vulnerable alone on the site – or perhaps alone but for some masked assailant, an opportunist seeking to steal rich pickings from anyone redeeming their possessions.

'OK, why not?' replied Danny, benevolent as ever. 'You can fill me in on the details along the way.'

3

SELF-STORAGE

'So, tell me all about these chess sets, Alice, and I'll offer you my best advice on how to dispose of them.'

As a keen chess player, Danny seemed to be looking forward to examining Steven's collection. I couldn't help hoping he might make a bid for one of them himself. One down, nineteen to go, maybe?

'Well, there are about twenty of them, in all shapes and sizes, some very fancy, such as the Alice in Wonderland set he once bought to try to win me over to yet another rabbit-hole of collecting that he'd started going down. No pun intended.'

'Did it work?'

I shook my head as I turned the car out onto the main road. 'I suppose I should have been more gracious as although he had a vested interest, he probably meant well. Maybe he'd just forgotten that I can't play chess. When I pointed that out, he said he thought it would make me want to take it up.'

When in his astonishment, Danny slammed his hand on

the dashboard, I had a flashback to my stressful driving test. That was the examiner's sign to do an emergency stop.

'You don't play chess? I never knew that.'

I shrugged. 'You never asked. To be fair, I did let Steven try to teach me, but it soon became clear that he didn't particularly enjoy the game either. He just liked the artistry of the tiny pieces. He liked ownership. I've always been thankful that most of his collections were of relatively small things, like egg-cups and stamps. It meant they didn't entirely swamp our house. But if you amass enough of even the tiniest object, you'll still end up with something huge.'

'Like atoms in a planet,' said Danny helpfully. 'Or drops of water in an ocean.'

I caught his eye in the rear-view mirror and gave a wry smile. 'Exactly. But I admit that some of his chess sets are beautiful and exotic. There's a stunning Indian one featuring intricately carved elephants and tigers and other jungle animals. And a handsome set from Peru, in which fierce-looking Incas play against Conquistadors.'

'I've always had a soft spot for the Isle of Lewis chessmen myself,' mused Danny. 'You know, those chunky little fellows carved from stone, named after the island in the Outer Hebrides where they were dug up. Although they weren't crafted by the islanders – they're generally believed to have Nordic origins. I think they were carved from walrus teeth or similar.' He grinned. 'Perhaps some passing Vikings left them behind.'

I laughed. 'I can't quite imagine marauding Vikings taking a chess set on board their longboats to while away tedious sea voyages on their way to a bit of pillaging. You'll be telling me next they always packed Travel Scrabble.'

'More likely whoever left them was taking the chess set

abroad to trade,' he replied. 'The Vikings traded as far afield as North America and Istanbul, although I think the Isle of Lewis chessmen have been dated a bit later than the Vikings. There are conflicting theories about their origin. But we digress. How valuable do you think Steven's chess sets are? Are there any antiques or rarities among them?'

I considered for a moment. 'He once told me he never paid more than a hundred pounds for any of them, but I never quite believed him. The truth will out now, as he's kept the receipts in each box to demonstrate their provenance. All will be revealed when I fetch them from his storage unit and inspect them.'

'Good idea. Because that way, you can make sure he's not been dealing in illegal sets.'

'Illegal? How can chess be illegal?'

In the rear-view mirror, I noticed him raise his eyebrows in expectation. Then I caught on.

'Oh, yes, of course, Ivory. Goodness, I hope none of them are made of ivory. That would be completely against the law.'

I know from our experiences at the museum that illegal trading in ivory was punishable by huge fines and even imprisonment, with very few exceptions, such as for licensed traders shipping to museums.

'Well, if he really did pay no more than a hundred quid per set, they won't be ivory,' said Danny. 'That'd be far too cheap.'

'Besides, he mostly bought them off eBay.' I turned right onto the lane that led to the edge-of-town industrial estate that housed Steven's self-storage warehouse. All the units on the estate, most of them to do with aspects of the motor trade, had already closed for the evening. The others were empty, plastered with battered *To Let* signs as if they'd been on the market for many months. 'I can't imagine people would openly trade in illegal ivory in such a public space.'

'You'd be surprised,' said Danny. 'Anyone can put any product description they like on an online retail site. What's to stop someone passing off an ivory chess set as bone or wood, or even resin or plastic?'

'The price differential,' I suggested. 'Surely no one's going to sell a genuine ivory set for the price of a plastic one?'

'Fraudsters? Money launderers?' said Danny. 'Smugglers trying to pass illegal goods to new owners by hiding them in plain sight? Who's to say the buyers aren't paying the difference some other way, e.g. ordering a hundred supposedly plastic chess sets at twenty quid each, knowing they'll be supplied with a single ivory set for two thousand pounds instead? Or whatever the black-market rate is these days.'

I stared into the distance, embarrassed at my naivete.

'Not that I'm suggesting for a moment that Steven was doing any of these things,' said Danny quickly. He is always so fair-minded.

'The obvious way to dispose of them would be to post them all on eBay again with "buy now" tags for fixed prices for the sake of speed,' he continued. 'But first things first, let's take a look at them and see whether any seem worth auctioning or taking to a specialist antique dealer. If it turns out they're all mass-produced and therefore have no rarity value, we can just go for a quick sale. I take it he left you with a key to his storage space?'

'It's all coded access these days,' I said. 'And I know the code. It's my birthday.'

I gulped at that admission. Plenty of my girlfriends complained that their partners never remembered their birthdays or anniversaries. That wasn't true of Steven. He wasn't all bad.

I hoped his shortage of cash wasn't putting him in any danger.

We drove on in silence for a few minutes before I said in a small voice, 'Danny, do you think if I'd taken more interest in Steven's collections, we'd still be together?'

Danny ran his hand over his mouth, considering.

'Let's look at this the other way round,' he said. 'Would you have loved him more if he'd taken up something to be like you? Knitting?'

'Of course not.' I gave a sheepish grin. 'You're right, Danny, thanks. He and I were very different people. Maybe opposites attract but not forever. It's just a shame it took us half our lives to work that out.'

Danny patted my hand where it lay on the steering wheel. 'Don't beat yourself up. You've started a whole new chapter now, and you're doing really well. But, if it makes you feel any better, why not give his chess sets a good send-off by using them to your own advantage in the meantime?'

I cringed. 'Please don't make me play you at chess with each set before we sell them. I'd rather lick the floor of the snug of The Quarrymen's Arms. I mean, I know you're good at chess, but—'

Danny sat back and raised his hands in mock surrender. 'No, don't worry. I'm not about to force myself on you.'

'Good thing none of the villagers are here to hear you say that. That's how rumours start.'

'What I mean is, you could put a chess-themed display in your shop window. It sounds as if there are some eye-catching ones you might use. And you never know, you might get higher offers from a passing tourist with holiday money to burn than from strangers bidding online.'

I felt my spirits lifting. 'I could even hold a special viewing afternoon, like a sort of test-drive for chess sets, in my shop. Although I'm not sure I've got enough flat space to display them all. Maybe we could hire the village hall instead and invite people to come along and try them out in a game. I've always felt bad because when Steven started collecting chess sets, I criticised him by saying they should be played with, rather than staying tucked away in their boxes all the time. I felt a bit hypocritical then saying I didn't want to learn to play chess with them myself.'

'Or you could use the school hall.' Ever practical, Danny refused to be drawn in by my self-pity. 'That would be a great way to encourage the village kids to take more of an interest in the game. They don't have much entertainment laid on outside the home here, compared to what city kids have.'

'Although urban kids don't have free access to all this beautiful countryside.' I took one hand off the wheel to gesture towards the fields and light woodland edging the lane. Raised as a city kid myself, I was surprised for a moment by my instinctive and heartfelt defence of my new community.

'Does the village school have a chess club, do you know?' asked Danny.

I locked eyes with him in the mirror, conspiratorial. 'I don't know, but if not, I have a feeling we're about to start one.'

4

RETRIEVING THE STOCK

As we drove up to the gated entrance, there was of course a security guard on duty in a little sentry box that everyone had to pass to gain admission to the site. I felt silly now for seeking Danny's protection.

I showed the guard an email from Steven granting me permission to access his unit, and he directed us to the most convenient entrance to the building to access it. It was on the other side of the building from the guard's office, out of his sight, although it was presumably included in the array of security camera feeds above his desk. When the guard returned to browsing a tabloid newspaper as soon as he'd checked our credentials, I was glad I had Danny with me after all. Security cameras are only of any use if a human being engages with them.

Danny hauled open the heavy door, which led to a long corridor whose floor, ceiling and walls were painted a sickly, fleshy pink. Each unit door was painted dark crimson.

I gulped.

'I feel like we're travelling down someone's alimentary canal,' I said.

We counted down the numbers as we approached Steven's unit.

'Here we are,' said Danny. 'Unit 976.'

I punched my birthdate into the electronic keypad on the door jamb and pushed open the door. I hadn't expected to feel so emotional at seeing Steven's stuff again. It was a graphic reminder of our failed relationship.

As we gazed at the stack of uniform boxes housing his things – I'd helped him pack them up, hence the methodical neatness – I remembered writing the labels on the outside, the scratchy sound of the marker pen against the rough cardboard, the pungent scent of its crow-black ink making my eyes water. At least, that was the excuse I made for the tears in my eyes.

I cleared my throat in an effort to pull myself together.

'What's the betting he's put his chess sets at the back of the unit,' I grumbled. I sniffed again. 'There's an awfully funny smell here.'

Danny inhaled deeply. 'What else do you think people store here? Dead bodies?'

I gasped, then he laughed.

'Oh, go on with you, I'm only joking. It just has that musty smell you get in the museum cellars. Nothing to worry about, I'm sure. Now, let's get on with the job in hand.'

The unit was as full as a Rubik's Cube, with boxes stacked from floor to ceiling. If anyone ever had the misfortune to be locked inside such a tightly packed storeroom, they'd run out of air to breathe within minutes. We started to remove the boxes at the front and set them down in the corridor to give us space to access these behind them. Soon, four cartons marked *chess sets* came into view, and we carted them out onto the corridor.

'I feel as if I'm stuck inside a video game,' said Danny, pausing to wipe his brow with the back of his hand. 'I'm half expecting the gaps in the stacks of boxes to be magically replenished as fast as we remove them.'

'Or for us to be crushed as they squash us against the wall.' I shuddered, thinking of similarly perilous scenes from vintage episodes of *Batman* and *The Avengers*. 'I'll go and load these in my car while you put the other boxes back, then let's get out of here. It's not a place I'd like to linger in.'

Danny turned the carton in his hands through a hundred and eighty degrees. 'I'll put them back with the labels facing us, to make it easier to find things if Steven needs you to flog any more of his stuff. By the look of this lot, you'll never be short of stuff to sell in your shop.'

His remark wrenched me back from my sad, nostalgic regret to the present, and to new opportunities.

Of course, my shop! This was the focal point of my life now, and the sooner we returned to it, the better.

Despite Danny's comforting presence, I still felt uneasy at the self-storage site, and couldn't stop myself from looking around as we pulled out of the car park, my spine prickling with the feeling that someone was watching me.

5

SETTING UP FOR PLAY

Back at the Curiosity Shop, we unloaded the chess sets from my car and stacked them up on the shop counter, ready to check they were all complete, and to examine any receipts and letters of provenance. We'd need a sales catalogue listing details of the stock, much as we produced exhibition catalogues at the museum. In many respects, years of service at the city museum had been excellent training for running my shop.

'I guess the sensible thing to do would be to catalogue them as we open them up, photograph each set so we have an at-a-glance reference guide, and keep the photographs with the paperwork separate from the actual sets,' Danny suggested. 'That should reduce the risk of pilfering, as the sets are going to be less valuable without proof of their provenance.'

'I feel a spreadsheet coming on,' I said with a grin.

Danny nodded approval. 'OK, let's get on with it.'

'Fine. How many pieces should there be in each set?'

Danny stared at me in disbelief. 'For goodness' sake, don't

say anything like that when you're trying to sell them, or your customers will think you know nothing and try to rip you off.'

I glanced at the nearest box, quickly counting the number of squares in a row: the board was eight by eight.

'Only kidding,' I said, although I wasn't. 'I know there are sixteen pieces.'

'Per side,' added Danny, giving me a knowing look. There wasn't much I could get past him.

'Exactly. Thirty-two pieces per set. That's what I meant.'

Danny pulled a high stool up to the counter and sat down. 'Actually, we shouldn't only count them, but make sure there are all the right pieces in each set. It would have been too easy to have mixed up a few sets while he was packing them away, and end up with no kings but four queens, for example.'

That made sense. I opened the first box and gently tumbled its contents onto the counter, before laying the box out flat, playing side up. Then I placed all the pawns in the second line in on each side, then began to sort through the more complicated pieces. Recognising the king and queen first, I set these on the central squares of the back row.

'Wrong way round,' said Danny, with a bemused smile.

He swapped them over. Considering the little horses and castles and the ones with a notch out of the top, I was thankful I'd started with a fairly straightforward set, rather than the one full of Incas and Aztecs.

Seeing me struggle, Danny jumped down from his stool and came to my rescue.

'I tell you what, I'll set them up, and you do the photos and paperwork.'

With a grateful smile, I pulled my phone out of my handbag and clicked on the camera icon.

A flurry of taps made us both look towards the shop door.

My heart skipped a beat. Had a would-be thief or mugger followed us home from the warehouse?

'Who would that be at this hour?' Danny asked.

To my relief, it was only Coralie, who was now pushing the door open. I must have forgotten to lock it after we'd brought the chess sets in from the car. I lifted the flap of the counter to go to welcome her.

'This is Coralie,' I said to him over my shoulder. 'You know, my new hairdresser friend I told you about? I don't think you've actually met her yet. Coralie, this is my friend Danny.'

'Doing a bit of late-night opening?' she asked, after greeting us both. 'I thought you closed at five.'

'Goodness, no!' I replied. It was so refreshing after working museum shifts to be able to determine my own working hours now.

'I hope you don't mind me walking straight in,' she said.

'Don't worry, you haven't interrupted anything. We've only just started.'

Coralie pointed at the chess sets on the counter. 'It looks like you've taken up chess with a vengeance,' she said, stroking the smooth, French-polished finish of the box on top of a stack of three.

I bit my lower lip. 'I'm afraid I don't even know how to play chess. These aren't mine. They all belonged to my ex, and he's asked me to sell them for him. We're just starting to do a stock-take before we arrange a selling exhibition in my shop here.'

Coralie opened the nearest set and extracted a chunky king from a reproduction of the Isle of Lewis chess set. Cradling him in the palm of her hand, she ran a forefinger over his carved features.

'He has a certain grumpy charm. He'd make a great salt cellar, don't you think, if you hollowed him out?' She tipped the king upside down and gave him a vigorous shake. 'Or maybe with a face like that, he should be the pepper pot, and the queen the salt. If you come across any odd pieces that don't fit in any sets, I'd be happy to take them off your hands and work my craft magic on them.'

Danny whisked the king out of her hand. 'Actually, we're hoping to sell them to people who will actually play chess with them.'

'Do you know any chess enthusiasts in the parish?' I asked, hopeful. Coralie seemed to know pretty much everyone in Little Pride, and as the local hairdresser, she was well-versed in village gossip.

As Coralie considered for a moment, she stroked the polished surface of one of the chessboards. 'If you count people who work in the village, I'd say your best bet is Jack Dauntless, who teaches at the school. I think the headmaster, Mr Wright, plays too, but Jack's much more fun. And better looking.'

I grinned. 'Jack Dauntless is a great name too. I can't wait to see what he looks like. I'm half expecting him to dress like the principal boy in a pantomime.'

'Who is traditionally played by a girl,' Danny reminded us. 'Is Jack short for Jacqueline, by any chance?'

'Oh no, Jack Dauntless is all boy all right. As an expert in compact living—'

'Coralie lives in a tiny house behind her salon – an old shepherd's hut,' I said for Danny's benefit.

'—I can't see how you could possibly display this many chess sets to advantage in your shop, especially if you're wanting people to play with them too.'

'I've already suggested that we approach the school to host the event,' said Danny. 'Having a chess enthusiast at the school already makes that seem an even better idea.'

In my excitement, I clapped my hands together. 'Brilliant! I'll get on the school's case first thing tomorrow.'

6

NEW PLAYERS

As promised, next morning, I phoned the school office and made an appointment to meet the headteacher, Mr Montgomery Wright, to float my proposition to him. I hadn't yet had any dealings with the school and had met only one teacher, Miss Blinken, very briefly, so I thought I might as well start at the top and let him delegate me to one of his staff if he wished.

On the phone, Miss Sally Pert, the school office manager, sounded as bright and breezy as her name. I asked for an early-morning meeting before my usual shop opening time of ten o'clock. She kindly booked me in for nine o'clock, the very start of the next school day.

* * *

It felt odd to be walking up the high street during the school run in among pupils careering along the narrow pavement on scooters and skateboards. Some of their parents escorting younger children had dogs on leads weaving in and out of the melee. I kept expecting them to trip up or entangle the children along the way, but long practice must have kept the kids immune to this obvious health and safety hazard.

Eavesdropping on snippets of conversation between the children and parents gave me an opportunity to gain insight into the school's community. I hoped this might help me pitch my event idea to Mr Wright.

'He may be Wright by name,' one woman was saying, with hair bleached to the same blonde as her Labrador, 'but he can't tell me how to raise my child.'

'Mr Tight, more like,' her friend replied between puffs of her vape. 'Told me if we can't afford to visit Florida in the school holidays, we shouldn't expect to take the kids out of school in term time to get the cheap prices.'

Her companion nodded. 'Doesn't know what "educational" means.'

Before I could find out what her personal definition of the word was, I was distracted by a sharp bump to my right heel. Turning round, I discovered a lanky boy of about ten stepping off the scooter whose front wheel had just grazed my foot.

He was clutching a mobile phone in his right hand to his chest, a fairground-style fanfare blaring from it, indicating his triumph in some kind of game.

'Sorry, miss,' he said, automatically addressing me as if I was one of his teachers. 'I did just win, though.'

As if that justified steering his scooter one-handed while staring at the screen, he gave an apologetic grin, clearly torn between celebrating his victory and worried about being told off. I guessed this kind of collision was a regular occurrence on the Little Pride school run.

As the school bell sounded in the distance, he fell into step with me, wheeling his scooter along beside him.

'So what game were you playing?' I asked, touched by his companionable manner.

'*Shred Fred*,' he replied cheerfully. 'And I'd just got my top score. I'd shredded my four hundredth alien into a fiery pit.'

My hand flew to my mouth. What a grisly victory, and so soon after breakfast too.

'That's not a game I know,' I replied. Then, hoping to prevent him from explaining it in detail, I continued, 'I'm more into traditional board games. Have you ever played chess?'

I hoped my bright tone would imbue the less antisocial game with the promise of enormous fun.

He shook his head as we strolled up the buggy-friendly slope to the school playground.

'Is it on Google Play, or just on iPhones? I'm only on Android at the moment.' He waved his phone at me by way of illustration. 'But Mum said I might get her old iPhone when I go up to big school next year.'

I wasn't entirely sure at first that he was being serious.

'You don't need a phone of any kind to play chess.'

He nodded sagely. 'Oh, I see, so it's on PlayStation.'

'Actually,' I began, wondering where to start, but I was saved the effort when my new friend – Herbie Studge, according to the name scratched on his handlebars – stopped to park his scooter in the bike rack. I was swept along by the crowd towards the playground wall, where I spotted a sign alerting me to a trail of blood-red footsteps on the ash-grey tarmac leading to the school office.

As I followed the footsteps, I couldn't help thinking

yellow or green might have been a more tasteful colour, and less ominous.

Just as I entered a narrow hallway with several doors leading off it, the door marked *School Office* opened, and Miss Blinken strode out, holding out in front of her a large black plastic bucket labelled *PHONES* in leaf-green paint. I turned to watch her take it out into the playground, where a queue of the older children quickly formed to drop their mobiles into the bucket, presumably where they had to stay until the end of the school day. Immediately, the noise level rose, as the children who had until now been silently transfixed by their phone screens began to chat to each other, shouting across the playground. A second bell silenced them as they formed into lines behind the class numbers painted on the playground. The old-fashioned discipline impressed me.

'Miss Carroll, I presume?' said a croaky, male voice behind me, and I realised I'd had an audience watching me watch the kids. He'd been standing in the school office doorway.

When I spun round to reply, I encountered a wiry man with round shoulders who would have been at least a couple of inches taller if he'd stood up straight. Beneath short, crinkly, grey hair, worry lines deeply etched his reddened skin. He looked like he'd pulled through hard times.

'Mr Wright?' I guessed, biting back a bad joke about having always wanted to meet my Mr Right. He looked too world-weary to deal with humour.

He led me through the main school office into what may once have been a broom cupboard, but now had an old-fashioned, double-pedestal desk and two ancient wooden chairs squeezed into it.

All three had seen better days. There were no windows, and not much on the desk, apart from a scratched aluminium name plaque declaring his name and title, a much-chewed pencil and some scrap paper. On the wall hung a framed graduate diploma, faded despite the lack of natural light, from a teacher-training college that I'd never heard of.

'My secretary tells me you want to hire the hall for a sale of chess sets,' he began without more ado. He looked almost cheerful at the thought. 'I used to play chess for my college in another lifetime.'

If the tiny office had had a window, at this point, he might have stared wistfully into the distance. As it was, he had to make do with eyeing the faded certificate as if it were a portal to a better place.

'I've been wanting to start a chess club here for years,' he continued. 'Only there's never any time. So much paperwork. I have to teach, too, since they cut our staff budget again for this academic year. Nor are there any chess sets on the premises, and no money to buy them. So, checkmate, you might say.'

He gave a hollow laugh, but at least it was a laugh of sorts.

I wondered what other dreams had been thwarted during his career. I felt bad for disappointing him.

'I'm sorry, I don't play myself, but I do have a lot of chess sets that I'd like to sell. I wondered whether I might use your school hall to host a chess afternoon to show them off to potential buyers. While some of the sets may be too fragile for the children to use, I'm sure there are several sets we could let them loose on during the afternoon. If you like, I could donate a couple of the less valuable sets to the school in lieu of paying a hire charge. You could use them to start a school chess club.'

When Mr Wright slumped back in his chair, I noticed one of its arms was missing.

Sensing I'd not yet won him over, I added, 'You could turn it into a school fundraiser if you like. Sell tea and cake. Run a raffle.' I knew already from my short time in Little Pride that both these things were staple features of village events. 'I gather one of your staff, Mr Dauntless, is a keen chess player, as is my friend Danny, who has volunteered to help on the day. He works at Broadwick City Museum, and he has the right safeguarding certificate clearing him to work with children. If we hold it at the weekend, you wouldn't have other duties to distract you, and you could even enjoy a nice game or two yourself.'

Mr Wright blinked a few times. Otherwise, his face remained expressionless. Then he perked up, leaning forward and thumping the desk so hard that his much-chewed pencil rolled onto the floor.

'Commission, too? Will you pay the school commission on sales?'

That thought hadn't occurred to me, but now he'd put me on the spot, I decided to offer a share of the reward I'd wangled from Steven. If I paid that to the school, I'd feel less exploitative for taking it off Steven in his hour of need. Plus, I'd still earn a decent cut for my shop.

'10 per cent,' I said quickly.

When he held out his hand, I almost expected him to spit on it before shaking on the deal, in classic schoolboy mode.

'Done,' I said brightly, wondering whether I had been.

Mr Wright scraped back his chair, pulling as far away from the desk as the tiny room allowed and leaning it on its back two legs.

If the kids did this in the classroom, I bet their teachers

would tell them off. Maybe this was his way of rebelling against the system, in the privacy of his own office.

'All four legs, if you please,' came a mature woman's sharp voice from the doorway. 'And Miss Pert is the office manager, not your secretary, remember.'

He gave a watery smile to the short, stout woman with a tight, grey perm above her mustard twin-set.

'Yes, Miss Boulder,' he replied meekly, returning the chair's front legs to the grubby carpet.

When she slapped the vacancies section of the *Times Educational Supplement* down on his desk, I wondered whether she was hinting that he should apply for a new position elsewhere, but he didn't seem to take offence.

Once she'd returned the way she'd come, her mission apparently completed, Mr Wright got up from his chair and held out his hand towards the door.

'I'll ask one of my team to contact you to confirm a date and time and to organise the event in detail,' he said grandly, as if he had a staff of thousands.

I hoped to goodness it wouldn't be the frightening Miss Boulder.

He followed me back into the main school office, where Miss Pert smiled sweetly at us both.

'Miss Pert, please take Ms Carroll's contact details and pass them on to Mr Dauntless,' he instructed. 'Now, if you'll excuse me, duty calls.'

He pushed past her and disappeared into the staff toilet along the corridor – an unusual definition of the word 'duty'.

'Yes, Mr Wright,' she replied, her wide, blue eyes twinkling. I wondered whether it was not willingness to please her boss or his visitor that had lit up her face, but the opportunity to liaise with Jack Dauntless, who I was now picturing as a swashbuckling, handsome hero in his prime.

Just then came a light tap at the door, and several children of various ages came in, each clutching a bag of plastic milk bottle tops. I'd seen a poster in Suki's Stores calling for donations of milk bottle tops in aid of the school roof fund. Initially, I pictured the children plugging holes in the leaky roof with the little coloured discs, but the poster told me a recycling company pays for them by weight. For all Suki's outward grumpiness, she always seemed to have some charity appeal going on in her shop.

Among the group of children was Tilly, Bob Sponge's granddaughter, who recognised me at once.

'Hello, Alice,' she cried, dumping her bag of bottle tops on Miss Pert's desk. She sprang towards me and threw her arms around my waist. 'What are you doing here? Have you come to be a teacher? That would be fun.'

I smiled, touched by her warm welcome. 'No, Tilly, sorry. I've just come to ask your headteacher whether I can use the school hall to run a special chess event. I've got lots of old chess sets to sell. He said yes. You and your friends and your families might like to come along and try some of them out. Would you like to learn to play chess?'

I thought I might as well start getting the word out about my event as soon as possible. I just hoped the kids would pass on an accurate message.

'Oh, I know all about chess,' said Tilly, waving a hand airily. Her friends looked impressed. 'The only thing is, if they're old sets, you'd better make sure you put new batteries in them first.'

I bit my lip to suppress a smile, and, beneath her ever-twinkling eyes, Miss Pert covered her mouth with a letter she'd just printed.

'Thanks, Tilly, I'll bear that in mind.'

Tilly gave a little skip of pleasure. 'Aways happy to help you, Alice.'

And with that, she trotted off down the corridor, chattering excitedly with her entourage.

7

JACK DAUNTLESS ADVANCES

A couple of evenings later, I was vacuuming behind the counter just after closing time when there was a knock at the door. At first, I assumed it was Danny arriving home from work, and that I'd inadvertently locked him out, but when I switched off the Dyson and looked up, my eyes met those of a handsome, neatly dressed fellow in beige chinos and a mauve shirt densely printed with tiny, white flowers. I guess he was in his early forties. *Not too young for me*, was the first thought that flashed through my mind. *Ha, you've got over your pining for Steven*, I admonished myself, glad to have shaken off the melancholy mood that had come over me in his self-storage unit.

'Come in, it's open,' I called, but I was thinking, *It takes a special brand of macho to carry off a pastel floral shirt.*

'Hi, I'm Jack Dauntless,' the stranger said in a soft, low Gloucestershire accent. 'Teacher at Little Pride Primary School. I hope you don't mind me stopping by without an appointment to have a word about your chess event, but I was just on my way home after a staff meeting, and I saw your shop lights were still on. If it's inconvenient, I can always make an appointment to come back another time, but Mr Wright said you were keen to set up the event sooner rather than later.'

I glanced at the wall calendar, thinking, *I bet some of your pupils' mums look forward to seeing you on parents' evenings.*

'Don't worry, now is just fine for me,' I replied, giving my best smile. I waved a hand towards the array of chess sets on the counter. 'Feel free to have a browse. We're just sorting out the sets to make sure all the pieces are there. Then we're going to choose a couple of the less fragile, cheaper sets for the children and other visitors to play with at the event. We'll set the rest up simply for viewing, and, with any luck, selling.'

Jack passed along the counter, picking up the odd piece and holding it up to the light for closer examination. For a tall, muscular type, he was surprisingly graceful.

'That is, if you think people won't feel shortchanged if they don't get to play with the more fancy sets?' I continued.

He set down the pale beechwood queen he'd been examining. Technically white, the pale wood was marbled with the colour of caramel ice cream.

'That's absolutely the right decision,' he replied. 'Serious chess players don't play with fancy sets, any more than bridge experts deal out fancy themed cards.'

That was another of Steven's addictions. Decks of playing cards featuring scenes from around the world, souvenirs of past holidays.

'Give the kids something indestructible,' he continued, turning over a delicately painted Alice in Wonderland wearing an oversized crown on her head. 'Much as they'd love playing with storybook sets like this.'

He bent over the counter to examine the jungle animals

in the next box without touching them. 'If this is a real antique, and not a cheap imitation, it could do well for you, if the right person comes along.'

'We've letters of provenance for the fancy ones,' I assured him. 'And receipts even for the cheaper, mass-produced sets. Hopefully, someone will want to buy those too.'

Jack considered for a moment. 'I'll drop a strong hint to the PTA that they might like to fund a few for school purposes. You'd think they'd be glad of the opportunity to introduce their kids to an offline, in-real-life game that doesn't involve phones. Our staff meeting just now was all about getting kids off their phones. They're not allowed them during the school day, of course, but we have no control over their use at other times, other than to try to tempt them to do more interesting things. Any idea when you'd like to run your event?'

'The sooner the better, really. Would before the end of September work for you?'

He wrinkled his perfect, straight nose. 'From past experience of school events, I suggest we make it in a month's time at least. So that takes us to the third Saturday in October. That will give us plenty of time to publicise it around the village and online.'

I was glad he said 'us'.

For a moment, I was torn. Danny would probably point out that it would be quicker to sell the chess sets on eBay, especially if we went for a fixed price rather than the auction option.

As Jack was checking the school calendar on his phone, the shop door opened again to admit Danny, now home from work.

'I'll just have to run the date past the Head before we can firm up on it,' said Jack.

'OK, that's fine by me,' I said, telling myself Steven was jolly lucky I was doing this at all, and it was perfectly fine to do it in my own time. I should not feel obliged to drop everything to suit him, when he'd ended our relationship with so little warning.

Danny hesitated in the doorway, grinning. 'Sorry, am I interrupting a romantic moment? I'll make myself scarce if you like.'

I pursed my lips, then said tersely, 'Danny, come on in and meet Coralie's friend, Jack Dauntless. He's just come to offer his services to help me sell the chess sets.'

When Jack flashed him a friendly smile, Danny marched across the shop floor to join us.

'Good man,' said Danny cheerfully, pumping Jack's proffered hand. 'I'll be helping too. I'm Alice's lodger. We're just friends, mind. I'd hate to give you the wrong idea.'

Was he really trying to set me up with Jack, having only just met him? Perhaps he had also noticed that what I'd mistaken for Robert's romantic interest in me seemed to have cooled off since Danny had moved in.

Not wanting to be distracted, I returned to the business in hand.

'So, Jack, I'll do some publicity around the village,' I continued, 'if you can spread the word within the school community and help us set up in the school hall on the day.' I glanced at Danny, who nodded eagerly. 'I'll make some posters to put up around the village too.'

'Don't forget the *Little Pride Parish News*,' said Jack. 'Around here, people's diaries are dictated by the events publicised in the *Parish News*.'

'Of course,' I replied, making a mental note to ask Suki who I should approach about it. The previous editor, Andrew Gloster, was currently on remand awaiting trial for the murder of the builder in the summer, and I didn't yet know who had been appointed as his replacement.

'I can approach the online chess groups that I belong to,' Danny offered.

'You might come across me on some of those,' said Jack, smiling encouragement. 'Message me where you've posted, and I'll make sure I like and share.'

He pulled a small notebook and pen out of the back pocket of his chinos, tore out a page and scribbled down his email address and phone number. Then he passed it to Danny, who murmured a thank you, and stood staring at it, as if trying to commit it to memory. For a moment, I thought he was going to put the scrap of paper in his mouth and swallow it, like a spy with secret instructions.

Jack glanced at the chunky sports watch on his wrist. 'Anyway, I'd better make tracks now. But I'm glad I caught you here – both of you.'

Danny stood up a little straighter.

'I'll drop you an email once I've cleared that date with Montgomery Wright, but I'm sure he'll be fine about it,' Jack added. 'Bye for now.'

'You're sure we can't tempt you to stop for a coffee?' Danny asked, although he knew as well as I did that for teachers, spare time is a precious commodity.

Jack shook his head. 'Sorry, it's been a long day, what with the after-school staff meeting, and I've got lesson prep to do for tomorrow. Another time, perhaps.'

With a smile and a wave, he headed for the exit. I waited until he'd closed the shop door behind him.

'Well, that's all good,' I declared to Danny. 'What a great team we are. Arranging this sale is turning out to be much easier than I'd expected. Thanks, Danny.'

Danny watched Jack stroll across the tea terrace before he replied.

'Thanks to Jack, you mean.'

I smiled. Danny's modesty had always been part of his charm. All I had to do now was chat up whoever had taken over the *Little Pride Parish News* to get the rest of the village on side, and I'd be on to a winner.

8

WELL VOLUNTEERED

Suki shouted from her post behind the till towards the far end of the village shop, 'Vicar, here's a volunteer for you to take over as editor of the parish mag, now that the old one's been banged up.'

'No, hang on, Suki,' I spluttered. 'I'm afraid you've got the wrong end of the stick.'

Suki gazed at me defiantly, her dark eyes alive with mischief. At least it made a change from her habitual sullen scowl.

Down by the delicatessen counter, the vicar, a tall, rangy figure in a dark suit and white dog collar, raised his hand in acknowledgement.

'Oh, Alice, how very good of you.' He beamed, peering over his half glasses at me and dropping a wedge of local cheese into his battered oilskin shopping bag. 'A fresh pair of eyes and a new pair of hands always benefits a parish project.'

I held up my hand in protest. 'Actually, I was only wondering who was running the *Little Pride Parish News* now that Andrew Gloster is, er, out of the picture?'

Suki pretended to busy herself reading a wildlife magazine on top of a pile of newly delivered periodicals, waiting to be shelved. But her eyes weren't moving, so I knew she was eavesdropping.

'How fitting it would be to see the magazine return to Nell Little's Cotswold Curiosity Shop, where she nurtured it for so many years.'

'Now Alice's Cotswold Curiosity Shop,' I corrected him, proud of the new sign I'd hand-painted the previous week.

I had the distinct feeling that the vicar was steamrollering over my objection.

'But I'm sure that would make her very happy,' I demurred. Nell Little had told me she hadn't wanted to give up her editorship when she still lived in Little Pride, but that Andrew Gloster had more or less forced her out, citing the frailty of her old age, so he could seize the power himself.

Power? What a pathetic fellow he was to have lusted after such a tiny empire, especially when it had required a great deal of hard work each month to compile, print and distribute the thing.

'Of course, you must sell the *Parish News* in your shop, as Nell did,' he continued, placing his basket on the counter. Suki began to ring up his purchases on the till. 'That's a perk of being the editor. Clever old Nell, such an easy way to lure people into her shop to pick up their copy, and interest them in her wares at the same time.'

'Oh, but I couldn't deprive Suki,' I said quickly, welcoming the chance to curry favour with the surly Suki. I would not like to be on the wrong side of her.

Proving that she had been listening in, Suki turned round. 'Doesn't bother me,' she said. 'I only took on selling it as a favour to the vicar, because Andrew didn't have a shop of his own to sell it in. People have to come in here anyway as it's the only food shop in the village. It'll stop me having to clutter up my shelf with the pesky collection box for it.'

'As you know, Nell's only a stone's throw away at Wendlebury Barrow if you need to ask her advice at all,' added the vicar. 'Not that I'm advocating throwing stones, ha ha. Let he who is without sin...'

I am too easily played.

'I suppose it would be good to have an excuse to visit her more often,' I said, which was true. 'I've been to see her a couple of times with Robert, and she was very kind to me. She must miss the social side of the shop.'

'And the local knowledge it brought her,' said the vicar. 'What with running the parish magazine and chatting to everyone who entered the Curiosity Shop, there wasn't much she didn't know about village life, until she went into the home, poor soul.'

His expression clouded over for a moment at the thought of such a dear old lady having to leave the hub of village where she'd lived her whole life. Then he brightened.

'Perhaps you might give her a formal role in the magazine, not only to help you, but also to bring the dear soul joy. I'm sure she would love to be asked to proofread the copy each month before it goes to print. She'd almost feel back at the heart of village life, and her spelling and grammar are impeccable.'

I gave a lopsided grin. 'Which is more than can be said for mine.'

'Two pounds twenty, please, Vicar,' said Suki, in an uncharacteristically courteous tone.

'Please put it on my account, my dear.'

Suki had already opened the customer account book at

his name. Out of the corner of my eye, I noticed a very long list of purchases in one column, with not a single payment recorded in the other. I couldn't imagine Suki being as lenient to any other villager. I'd recently seen her publicly name and shame a young man in the village for being overdue on settling his monthly account worth less than a fiver.

The vicar turned to me, beaming as he held out his right hand. Without thinking, I reached out to shake it.

'So that's a deal.'

Suki turned away to conceal her smirk.

'I'll drop the files around to you this afternoon. Andrew arranged for them to come to me before he left, so I can give you everything you need.' He picked up his basket. 'Poor Andrew. Love the sinner, hate the sin,' was his parting shot as he left the shop with a cheery wave.

Suki turned back to face me, shaking with what had been silent laughter but now morphed into raucous mirth.

'Thanks, Alice,' she chortled. 'You couldn't have timed your visit better. The vicar had come in here with the intent of persuading me to take on that pesky rag. Me! Can you imagine me in charge of the *Little Pride Parish News*?'

I joined her laughter at the concept, admiring her self-awareness. In Suki's hands, the magazine would soon morph into a biting satire of village life. A lot of people might like to read Suki's version, but the legal bills to defend her libel would bankrupt the shop in no time.

She pushed towards me the diminishing pile of the September issue of the *Little Pride Parish News*. Then she extracted the collection tin for *Parish News* payments from among a huddle of donation boxes for various animal charities. The villagers' pounds for their copies were kept separate from Suki's till and were collected and banked each month,

Nell had told me, by the parochial church council's treasurer, Matthew Ironbridge.

'You owe me, Suki Price,' I said under my breath as I left the shop. Of course, I knew I could have said no, and as I strode back down the high street to my cottage, I realised I had only myself to blame. I just hoped this new responsibility would bring me worthwhile benefits.

9

FAIR SHARES

Next morning, during a quiet spell in the shop, I'd got stuck into reading the *Parish News* files that the vicar had dropped round on a memory stick the previous evening, perhaps eager to make me commit to the position of editor before I could back out. I was thankful the files included a template for the magazine, presumably created by Andrew. I doubted Nell Little, at her age, had used such technology, especially considering the till in the shop was an ancient mechanical one.

A soft tap at the shop door made me look up. To my surprise, it was old Maudie Frampton. Usually, she announced her presence by kicking the door with her husband's hobnailed boots. Her gentler approach today was a pleasant surprise.

As she crossed the threshold, I discovered the reason: the strength of her kick had been muted by a large pair of red tartan bedroom slippers in place of her usual footwear. Noticing me looking at them, she said quickly, 'Me husband needed his boots today.'

'Ah, right,' I said, as if it were perfectly usual for husband

and wife to share their footwear. I'd never hankered after wearing Steven's brogues or biker boots any more than he'd fancied my habitual Mary-Janes.

The slippers were fraying across the instep, and one of the pom-poms was missing. This was no fashion statement, but a necessary choice. How poor did a couple have to be these days to share a solitary pair of outdoor shoes? Remembering that Maudie had spent five pounds on a velour hat she probably couldn't afford at my opening event back in the summer sent a frisson of guilt through me. It was a smart vintage hat, and the price would have been a steal in a city-centre vintage clothes shop, but hardly an essential purchase for someone so hard up. Now I wondered what Maudie had sacrificed in order to support my shop.

This was indeed a village of contrasts. Next door to me lived a multi-millionaire, while our neighbour here couldn't afford her own pair of shoes. While sad for Maudie and her husband, I liked Little Pride all the more for its mixed community. It seemed more genuine somehow, unlike nearby Great Pride, where Robert's daughter lived. Great Pride was dominated by wealthy locals and weekenders from London.

I decided that the next thing she brought to sell me in the shop, I'd find an excuse to give her at least five pounds more than it was worth, so that her kind hat purchase hadn't left her out of pocket. With perfect timing, she produced a battered vintage toffee tin from her basket and set it on the shop counter. When I expressed delight at the retro design of the tin – it looked mid-century – she picked it up and shook it with vigour. It made a noise like maracas.

'I've brought it to sell the contents rather than the tin,' she declared, eyeing me hopefully.

With thumbs thickened and bent by arthritis, she prised

off the lid to reveal at least a hundred buttons of all shapes and sizes, many at least as old as their container.

In the top layer, the facets of a chunky black glass button cut like a carnation glinted in the autumn sunshine. I picked it up, genuinely admiring the design, and dropped it into the open palm of my left hand. It was surprisingly heavy where it lay. As I ran my fingers through the tin to examine the variety of its contents, I noticed Maudie was breathing rather fast.

'Are you OK?' I asked.

Now that I looked at her, she seemed unusually pale, and her mouth hung open as she panted hoarsely, 'Just a little weary, my dear. Forgot to take my pill this morning.'

It was the first time she'd called me 'my dear'. That felt like a breakthrough. When I moved in, I'd been slightly afraid of her. Now I realised how vulnerable she was. Her usually gruff manner couldn't mask her physical frailty.

'Let me get you a chair,' I said, setting down the button box beside the till.

I dashed out from behind the counter to haul across to her a pine carver chair. She sighed with relief as she lowered herself into the seat.

'You're too young to remember this, but when I was a young 'un, there was a campaign in local shops to provide a chair for the oldies. "We care with a chair" was the slogan, and my granny was so grateful she'd sit in every shop chair she came across, whether she needed to or not. Took her forever to get her shopping done.' She chuckled fondly as she gazed into the distance. 'Never thought I'd be needing one meself.' She narrowed her eyes. 'Take my advice, my dear. Never get old.'

I gave an awkward grin.

'Well, it beats the alternative,' I quipped, and was relieved to see her smile.

She sat back and closed her eyes, and I wondered whether she was about to nod off or, God forbid, to breathe her last. A dead body in the shop would not be good for business, even if due to natural causes. Or perhaps it would around here. Villagers seemed to love a bit of intrigue. I supposed as the new editor of the *Little Pride Parish News*, I'd have to report any such incident. Would it also fall to me to write an obituary?

As Maudie emitted a faint snore, I came to my senses. Perhaps she was just tired. A power nap might revive her. But I patted my pocket to check my phone was there, just in case I should suddenly need to call an ambulance. I took the opportunity to check through her button box before naming a price. Carefully, so that none of the buttons would spill onto the floor, I tipped the contents onto the counter and spread them out into a single layer, the better to assess them.

Immediately, I recognised the collection was a treasure trove to a keen knitter like me. Distinctive buttons make such a difference to a handknitted garment or accessory. And if there were any there that I couldn't use for my needlework, Coralie would surely snap them up for one of her many craft projects. I guessed the collection of vintage buttons had been in Maudie's possession for decades, and perhaps in her family for generations, harking back to the days when every woman knitted all the family's woollens, from vests to socks, and frugally cut off the buttons from outgrown or worn-out garments to re-use.

I bet Maudie's grandmother could have taught us a thing or two about recycling. I wondered whether Maudie had any rag rugs her ancestors had made from old clothes. I wouldn't have minded a few of these in my shop – they'd be snapped up by fans of cottagecore. I fancied trying to make one myself.

As I swept the buttons back into the tin, the pattering sound, like gentle rain, disturbed Maudie from her slumber. Her head jerked back, and she opened her eyes, looking around as if trying to remember where she was. I pretended not to have noticed she'd nodded off. When she licked her lips, I guessed she might be thirsty or even dehydrated.

'Actually, Maudie, I was just about to make myself a pot of tea,' I said, trying to sound casual. 'There'll be plenty in the pot for a cup for you too, if you'd like one? On the house,' I added quickly, seeing her hesitate, perhaps wondering how much I charged for hot drinks. 'In fact, you'll be doing me a favour. Otherwise, I'll only drink the whole pot myself and have to keep nipping to the loo all afternoon.'

She sat up a little straighter. 'Oh well, in that case I'll be glad to help you out.'

When I fetched a plate of biscuits and set them beside on the counter, I was gratified to see her tuck in, dunking them enthusiastically in her tea.

'So, these buttons,' I began. 'I take it you'd like me to sell them for you?'

I'd kept to Nell Little's long-established arrangement of selling items for villagers on commission. No money changed hands until I'd sold them, and if they didn't sell within a certain time, the owner was obliged to take them away.

When I'd first realised this was expected of me, I'd been horrified, fearing being exploited, but in practice, it worked well. It kept the contents of my shop fluid and interesting without my having to tie up a lot of cash I didn't have in stock.

'If you wouldn't mind, my dear,' said Maudie. 'I've no more use for them now my hands have got too stiff to sew.'

She splayed out thick, arthritic fingers. Her thinning wedding band, its surface a mesh of scratches from long wear, cut in tightly to her ring finger. She couldn't have been able to remove it for a very long time. 'I've told Frampton if he loses a button now, he'll have to make do with a safety pin.'

She drained her cup of tea, and I topped it up from the pot. I'd used an especially large pot to ensure there'd be enough for seconds. She helped herself to milk and two sugars, stirring them in vigorously until the liquid spun like a whirlpool.

'So, can you sell 'em or not?' she asked, taking another biscuit. 'Them buttons.'

'Actually, I'd like to buy them from you for myself. I do a lot of knitting. Or rather, I used to until I came here. They'd come in very handy for all sorts of projects. In fact, they'd inspire me to get out my needles and wool again, especially now we're moving into the cooler autumn weather. It'll be a lovely cosy activity, and I can easily do a few rows in odd moments while I'm sitting behind the counter here.'

Maudie nodded her approval. 'The devil makes work for idle hands.'

So, I hadn't entirely redeemed myself in her eyes yet. I suppressed a smile. 'I'll give you the money for them in cash straight away if that's OK?'

Maudie pursed her lips in thought. 'I was thinking ten pence a button? There's a hundred and seven of 'em. Frampton counted 'em while I was making his porridge this morning. And a pound for the tin?'

'Oh, Maudie, they're worth more than that. Some of these buttons are little works of art.'

She shrugged her shoulders. 'I don't think there's

anything special there, just old-fashioned wood and glass and plastic.'

I was sure I'd seen some Bakelite too, and at least one Venetian-style *millefiori*. Had any of her ancestors travelled that far afield, perhaps serving in the military during the war? Or maybe they'd been in service and had fancy items handed down by their employers.

'Even so, they're pretty to the modern eye, and nice retro designs are very fashionable these days,' I said. 'I'd be hard-pressed to find buttons like that locally, even in the haberdashery at John Lewis in town. So, would you take thirty pounds for the lot?'

Maudie did a double take. 'If you let me give you the tin for free,' she offered, and I did my best to look as if I'd got the better bargain – which, to be honest, was probably true.

The rustle of six crisp five-pound notes in her hand perked her up even more than the tea and biscuits. She tucked them in an ancient tweed purse, which she stuffed back into her coat pocket.

'That's very good of you, my dear, and I appreciate the tea and biscuits and the chair.' She patted one of its arms as if thanking the chair too.

'You're very welcome.' I smiled. 'And thank you for telling me about the "caring with a chair" campaign. It's a very good idea. In fact, I'll keep the chair there for other customers to use, so come in and use it any time you like.'

She set both hands on the arms of the chair to raise herself to her feet, and stood for a moment taking in the scene, perhaps picturing future visits. If she brought me something like the button box every time and told me more of her memories, that would be fine by me. I was already itching to get knitting again. I might even start my own vintage button collection. Whatever would Steven think after I'd complained so often about his acquisitions?

As she turned to go, Robert entered the shop, bearing another bunch of roses from his garden, this time unusual blooms marbled in deep pink and white, reminding me of raspberry ripple ice cream.

Maudie turned back to me, steadied herself with one hand on the counter and lowered her voice.

'Look out, here comes Bob Sponge, trying to buy his way into your affections. Don't you fall for it, my dear. As Frampton used to say when he was courting me, "share and share alike". That's the secret of our very long marriage – sixty years come February. For richer, for poorer, is what we vowed on our wedding day. But one rich, one poor is a recipe for strife. You just remember that.'

Robert, sensing Maudie was confiding in me, had the tact to linger near the window, examining a brass letter-rack with exaggerated interest.

'Still, I suppose he'd be better than someone like that Andrew Gloster. I never did take to him. Eyes too close together, if you ask me. I don't know how he ever got picked to be a spy.'

She clearly still believed the rumour put about by Andrew Gloster himself, faking a more intriguing and glamorous back story than his actual accountancy career.

As Maudie reached the door, Robert approached and held it open for her with old-fashioned courtesy, allowing her to exit.

'Mr Sponge,' she said louder, nodding in greeting as she brushed past him.

'Mrs Frampton.' He returned the nod. Then he strolled

across to the counter, placing the roses beside the button box, whose lid I hadn't yet replaced. He peered into the tin.

'Don't tell me Maudie Frampton's been paying you in buttons?' he said. 'I knew she was hard-up, but didn't think things had got that bad for her.'

'Actually, you could call it currency exchange,' I replied. 'I've just bought them off her to use myself. They're mostly vintage and gorgeous. You don't get buttons like these any more. She's inspired me to get my knitting out, if only to provide a vehicle for her beautiful buttons. I could easily knit things for the shop, in my spare time, whether garments or household accessories such as tea cosies and cushions decorated with Maudie's buttons.'

Robert raised his eyebrows. 'That's a new one on me. I'd heard you were setting up a chess shop.'

I clapped my hands to my cheeks in mock horror. 'You can't do anything round here without the whole village knowing. Who told you that?'

'Tilly.'

That didn't seem quite so alarming. At least his granddaughter had got the story from me first hand, even if it had lost a bit in translation.

'Not quite. But I will be displaying some chess sets in my shop to promote a chess event and sale I'm organising at the village school. You should see posters going up about it around the village later this week, once I've made them, and there'll be more details in the October *Parish News*.'

'Ah yes, the vicar told me you'd volunteered as editor.'

I gave a hollow laugh. 'Hardly. But I thought Nell Little would be pleased. I'm going to ask her advice about it. I'll also restore her history of the village that Andrew Gloster axed when he took over. Actually, I'm thinking of going to see her after I close for lunch. Or I could go this evening, but I don't like being out when Danny gets home. Would you like me to take these roses over for her? I presume that's who they're for.'

Robert looked down at the bouquet.

'Ah, yes, Danny,' he said levelly. 'Of course.'

Then I clapped my hand to my forehead. 'But what am I thinking? I can't go until he gets back because he's got the car.' My car, actually, as there was no public transport to town from Little Pride, but I seldom needed it during opening hours. I shook my head at my own foolishness.

Robert brightened.

'Well, I'm happy to run you across to see her whenever you like,' he said. 'In fact, I was planning to take these to her today anyway. Pick you up at one?'

'Perfect,' I said. 'If you like, I'll stick these in some water to keep them fresh here till then. They'll look lovely on the counter in the meantime, and their fragrance is intoxicating. Lucky Nell.'

'Yes, lucky Nell, indeed,' said Robert, and he turned to go.

10

TEAMWORK

'I hear he's all yours, my dear,' said Nell.

'What?' I shot a confused look at Robert, who lowered his eyes and bit back a smile. Then I realised what Nell meant.

When I first moved to Little Pride, it took me a while to get used to the way villagers of her generation often used personal pronouns to refer to inanimate objects. Somehow, my news about my appointment as editor of the *Parish News* had reached Nell before I had.

'Congratulations,' Nell was saying, her beady eyes darting back and forth between Robert and me. 'I'm very glad to hear that the magazine is back in responsible hands, after that rogue Andrew Gloster took it over.'

I wrinkled my nose. 'I fear your confidence may be misplaced, Nell,' I said. 'Although I've settled into my new home, I still have very little knowledge of local events and traditions, and there are loads of people in the village that I haven't even met yet. I don't want to let them down.'

When Nell steepled her bent fingers, I had a feeling she was about to offer wise counsel. 'All the more reason to take the job on, then. It'll be a crash course in village life, and those you don't yet know, you soon will. They'll have to get to know you if they want to keep in with the new editor.'

More of a baptism of fire, I thought to myself, but her point was a good one.

She turned to Robert and reached out her hands. 'Dear boy, are those for me?'

He laid the roses gently onto her lap.

'Mind the thorns,' he added.

I suspected it would take more than a few thorns to deter Nell from what she wanted. She brought the blooms to her nose and breathed deeply to absorb their musky smell. Sighing with contentment, she lowered them to her lap.

'Heavenly,' she declared. 'And all the more so as it's been so long since you last brought me your roses. Nothing compares to home-grown village flowers. The supermarket kind that most visitors bring smell mostly of the plastic wrapper.'

I shot him a sideways glance of concern. Was her short-term memory fading? He'd brought her those beautiful apricot roses only the week before. Or at least, when he brought them into my shop, he told me he'd picked them for her. Was he dating another woman somewhere and just wasn't ready to go public about her yet?

'So, to what do I owe the pleasure of your visit this time?' Nell asked. 'Not that you need an excuse to stop by. You'll always be welcome here.'

'Actually, it was the *Parish News* that I came to see you about,' I explained. 'I wanted to ask if you'd any advice. The vicar's handed all the archives over to me, and I shall look through back issues from your tenure, but it would be great to speak to you about it in person to pick up any tips you can give me.'

'I'd be obliged if you'd put my village history column back in,' she said at once. 'It should still be there in the archives.'

I smiled. 'That was already part of my plan.'

'Well, come again and ask away, any time you like,' said Nell, her eyes twinkling. 'You will always find me at home. But you're in charge now, so make you own rules to suit yourself. Don't let anyone else stand in your way. If anyone else thinks they could do a better job, tell them they're welcome to try it, and they'll soon back off. And how is the shop running? Any questions there?'

I hadn't planned to quiz her about the Curiosity Shop for fear of overtaxing her with too many questions at once, but now I was grateful for her offer.

'I'd welcome your advice about pricing some chess sets I'm selling for a friend as a favour. I want to do right by him, but I don't want to give them away at foolhardy prices.'

Nell tapped her thin lips with a bony forefinger. Her deeply ridged fingernails were newly polished in a rose pink. 'To be honest, my dear, I just followed my instincts. The best price is the most anyone is prepared to pay. That depends how much a person wants a piece. Sometimes that can be much higher than the item is worth to anyone else.'

Maudie Frampton's button box sprang to mind.

'There may be times when a customer tries to beat you down,' Nell continued. 'But stand your ground unless you have a genuine reason to negotiate. I'll give you a cautionary tale. Once a pleasant fellow spent a long time admiring an antique Persian rug, one of several items I'd acquired from a local estate clearance, as the heir didn't care for them and couldn't be bothered to find a buyer. I insisted on paying what

I thought a fair rate, so as not to take advantage. In the case of the rug, it was fifty pounds, and I was confident of selling it at a mark-up of at least 50 per cent.'

'Seventy-five pounds,' interjected Robert, only to be quelled by Nell's hard stare. Nell may not have been familiar with the term 'mansplaining', but she'd doubtless experienced it enough times.

'The man lingered a while,' she continued, 'admiring the pattern and quality of the rug, before leaving the shop to think about it, returning a couple of hours later. He'd decided he must have it but couldn't afford my asking price. Would I accept fifty pounds? I did my best shocked look, pressing for seventy pounds, then sixty-five. When he shook his head and turned to go, saying it was beyond his budget, his whole body oozed sadness. His shoulders bent, he dragged his feet and stared at the floor as he trudged towards the door, sapped of all interest in any other aspect of life.

'Well, of course, my heart went out to him. He'd clearly appreciated the rug more than the estate's heir had done, and provided I got what I paid for it, what did it really matter if I made no profit? My reward would be the pleasure of transforming his misery to joy. I called after him: "It's yours for fifty pounds, sir." He spun on his heel and positively sprinted towards me, calling me every gracious name under the sun. When he paid me in cash, with five much-creased ten-pound notes, I wondered how long he'd been saving up to treat himself.

'"If you bear with me a moment," he said, "I'll fetch my car to the front of your shop and load the rug on the back seat to keep it pristine."

'I assumed his boot was full of other stuff – the tools of his trade as a gardener or a mechanic perhaps – and that he didn't want to dirty the rug.

'Imagine my astonishment when a moment later, a gleaming Bentley pulled up outside. I dashed to the front door – I could still dash in those days – to ask the driver to move along, to make space for my customer. But as I opened the shop door, my carpet-buyer stepped out of the front passenger seat. A peak-capped chauffeur was at the wheel. Oblivious to my astonishment, he skipped back inside to roll up the carpet and carried it out to his car without a word of explanation. That was the last time I let myself be beaten down to cost price. May you learn from my error, my dear.' She gave a self-deprecating smile. 'But in truth, I never really lost sleep over the prices I charged. All I needed was enough to get by, and to me that was worth as much as any riches.'

Robert cleared his throat, perhaps taking her comment as criticism. Not that he had anything to feel guilty about, as far as I knew. He may have been the richest man in the village, but I'd heard tell of his philanthropic ventures, many of which were documented by the media and listed in less hysterical tones on his company website.

I decided to bear Nell's advice in mind when pricing Steven's chess sets: not so high as to be greedy, but low enough to sell without delay.

The grandfather clock in the care home's lobby struck the quarter before two, and I jumped to my feet. It was time to get back to work at the shop compiling the October issue of the *Little Pride Parish News* to spread the word about my chess event.

11

PRESSING ON

By the second week in October, I was feeling pleased with myself. I'd published my first issue of the *Little Pride Parish News*, which was ably proofread by Nell. To my amazement, she didn't even need reading glasses. It included the cute poster I'd designed to announce my event, which I'd calculated to appeal to all ages and levels of skill in chess.

Copies were selling at what Suki assured me was the usual pace – the bulk of purchases in the first week of the month, followed by a steady trickle from those who'd either lost track of the turning of the calendar or mislaid their original copy and needed to replace it.

I'd also pinned copies of the poster on public noticeboards, in Suki's Stores, Coralie's Curls, The Quarrymen's Arms and at the bus stop, and I'd stapled a few to telegraph poles about the village for good measure. I'd discovered this was still one of the most effective ways of spreading news in Little Pride, even in our digital age. I'd also managed to get a picture in the local paper, with images of some of the most interesting sets – an affordable Isle of Lewis reproduction and a more valuable Indian elephant set – on display in my shop window.

Danny and Jack had been working in tandem to spread the word online among special interest groups and chess-related websites. I was grateful to them for working so hard on my behalf. They even met in the pub a couple of times a week to agree their strategy, monitor progress and dream up new promotional ideas. Jack had also disseminated the details among the pupils and their families via the school's e-newsletter.

Danny had surprised me by volunteering to take his regular Wednesday afternoons off (time in lieu for working at the museum some weekends) to help with Jack's chess club for the schoolchildren once it was up and running. Although I was touched that Danny was being so generous with his time, it made me realise he was making a long-term commitment to staying in Little Pride. I'd assumed taking him in as my lodger was merely a temporary solution to his need to move out of Martin's flat in a hurry.

Not that he was any trouble. I enjoyed his company, and his rent money was a handy supplement to my monthly income while I was still building up the shop's earnings.

On the other hand, I only had one spare bedroom, which I'd need for my mum whenever she came to stay. At the age of seventy-five, she could hardly be expected to doss down on the sofa.

I'd resolved after splitting up with Steven to see more of her – she'd never really liked Steven, and, unfairly, blamed him that we'd been unable to provide the grandchildren she'd longed for. I never confessed to her and Dad that the tests we'd been through had shown the deficiency was in me, not Steven, and that our only hope had been IVF. It took me a while to build up the courage to try. Although Steven's part in the process would have been relatively easy, I was scared of so much medical intervention on my body and wellbeing.

We had three failed attempts at IVF before I insisted we admit defeat. After all, we had so much else in our lives to be thankful for, and I didn't want the strain of the process to drive us apart. So much for that idea.

Looking back, I realise now I should have told Mum and Dad the whole story. They would surely have understood. Instead, to my continuing regret, I'd allowed the unspoken issue to drive a wedge between us. Now it was too late to make amends with Dad, as he'd passed away a few years before, but at least he hadn't had to know that Steven and I had split up in any case.

Was it too late now to rebuild my relationship with Mum? At the age of fifty, I was clearly too old to give her any grandchildren. She would know that too, and perhaps that would help her come to terms with it and move on – not that she had any real choice.

Since I'd parted from Steven, I'd realised how much I had missed her, and how isolated she must have felt since Dad died. Perhaps if I tried really hard now, I could be reconciled with Mum and even make up for lost time. I should set a date for her to stay, and then give her my undivided attention, showing her how happy I was in my new way of life.

Even with Danny lodging here, I could still set a date for her stay, and I could sleep on the sofa while she took my room. I couldn't expect Danny to sacrifice his bed for her when he was paying me monthly rent, and if, with his characteristic generosity, he offered, I'd have to be firm and refuse.

All these thoughts were whirring round my head as I

opened the shop the morning before the sale of Steven's chess sets at the school, as well as the launch of Chessmates, which was what, at Jack's suggestion, the school had decided to brand the new club – a clever combination of the notion of victory in chess ('checkmate!') and the social aspect of the club. Now in an established routine for opening and closing the shop, I was operating on autopilot. I barely broke my stride as I turned the shop door sign to *Open* and flung open the front door to let in the fresh, autumn, morning air.

But then I stopped in my tracks, distracted by some unexpected red marks on my patio. Surely graffiti artists didn't target sleepy Cotswold villages? Didn't they stick to urban sites like railway arches and road bridges?

But this was not the chunky, colourful tag of a city-dwelling anarchist. It was a message spelled out in even lettering, and it wasn't aimed at passers-by. The neatly spaced words were painted to face me as I looked out from the shop:

IVORY TRADERS HAVE BLOOD ON THEIR HANDS

That's random, was my first thought. I didn't disagree with their sentiment, but why would anyone direct something like that at me? Why here?

Cross at having the neat, stone slabs of my tea terrace defaced, I fetched a bucket of water from the kitchen and splashed it all over the lettering. I repeated the process twice more, until all that remained of the message was a pale-pink wash trickling down to the gutter beyond the pavement. Its quick dispersal was further evidence that it wasn't the work of an experienced graffiti artist, whose favoured medium was aerosol spray paint. From the shining surface of the letters, and the tangy aroma, I guessed this vandal had preferred to use a squeezy bottle of tomato ketchup – far easier to source in the village than spray paint, being stocked in Suki's Stores.

12

UNEXPECTED ITEM IN THE TEA AREA

I was ready to dismiss the message as an eccentric prank by an early riser, until, on re-entering the shop, I noticed the elephant chess set taking pride of place in the window.

My stomach churned, and I closed my eyes. Was I trading inadvertently in poached ivory? The very thought filled me with horror.

A few months before, while browsing Facebook, I'd had to click away from a gory post campaigning against the illegal ivory trade, showing after-photos of elephant poachers' victims. Did anyone around here really believe that I would be complicit in such an awful act by selling ivory goods in my shop?

No, it was ridiculous. Just because that set was carved into the shape of elephants didn't mean they were carved from their tusks, any more than my fluffy panda onesie was made from real panda fur.

My head swimming, I staggered back a couple of paces and almost fell into one of the patio chairs, noisily knocking over a round, metal tea table and smashing the plant pot filled with herbs that stood on it. At that sound, Robert's front door flew open, and I heard footsteps crunching across the gravel on his front drive. The high wall between our properties shielded whoever it was from my view, but I rather hoped it was Robert.

Sure enough, a few seconds later, Robert came charging along the pavement and onto my tea terrace. Seeing my obvious distress, he rushed up the path and set the fallen table upright.

I knew Robert was a keen environmentalist. His highly successful business was built on inventing the everlasting washing-up sponge, saving tonnes of plastic being produced and disposed of. He had also rehomed the pair of donkeys that had lived on the paddock beside my cottage before I moved in when a builder bought the plot and wanted rid of them. But I couldn't imagine Robert would go in for shock campaign tactics like this.

To be honest, Robert had seemed a little distant since Danny had moved in, dashing my hopes that we might get to know each other better after working together to solve the murder in the summer. In idle moments, I'd even begun to consider whether we might ever be more than neighbours. Then I'd chide myself for being presumptuous. The man was a millionaire who travelled the world with his highly successful business. He was hardly likely to fall for his next-door neighbour.

In times of crisis, it is astonishing how many diverse thoughts can go through your mind simultaneously. It's as if time slows down by several orders of magnitude. Whether the brain speeds up or time slows down, I have no idea – but one or both of those factors applied now as I watched Robert stride across the terrace towards me.

He crouched down in front of my chair and rested both hands gently on my shoulders.

'Alice, are you OK? I heard the clatter and assumed one of your customers had come to grief on the tea terrace. I saw Maudie Frampton tottering past earlier looking a bit peaky. I feared she'd fallen over on her way home, cannoning sideways across your patio furniture.'

I raised a hand to my damp brow. 'No, sorry, that was just me being clumsy.' My voice was hoarse. 'I've just had a shock.'

When Robert followed my pointing finger to my pink-tinged patio, his brow furrowed. 'Sorry, Alice, what is it exactly that you can see there?'

Oh no, now he thinks I'm hallucinating. I groaned inwardly. This wasn't helping my cause.

'Oh well, it's gone now, I washed it away. But earlier there was a message there, written in ketchup, accusing me of trading in ivory.'

'And are you?' he said evenly.

'No, of course not!'

He took a step back and sat down in the empty chair at my table, before lifting the terracotta pot of thyme that stood at its centre. Now that the wildflowers in my back garden were over, I'd put potted herbs on every table instead of home-grown posies. From beneath the pot, he pulled out a leaflet printed in bright green, red, white and black.

'They seem to have left you a more formal campaign leaflet too,' he observed, glancing at its front and back.

'What, for the parish council elections?' I squealed. 'I know they're coming up soon, and that they're likely to be fiercely fought, but do they usually cause blood to be spilled? Or rather, fake blood. What kind of parish council candidate leaves offensive graffiti on his constituents' doorsteps?'

Robert bit back a smile. 'Not an electoral campaign, Alice. A pro-wildlife campaign. Anti-poaching. Against the ivory trade. I doubt it's the work of the local anti-fox-hunting brigade, though that could be a good starting point for enquiry if you decide to investigate.'

The local hunt met regularly at the end of our village, where a couple of campaigners were always waiting to greet or them with home-painted signs saying, *Stop the hunt* and *Let foxes live*.

'Mind you,' he continued, 'I don't suppose the two groups are entirely mutually exclusive. If you're anti-fox-hunting, you're likely keen on preserving other wildlife and animal rights too.'

'So, what does the leaflet say exactly?' I asked.

'"Stop elephant poachers – end ivory trading now".'

Now I was starting to rally a little in the wake of Robert's chivalric arrival, time had resumed its normal steady pace.

'There are two major flaws in the culprit's logic,' I said slowly. 'First of all, ivory trading has been illegal in this country for decades. I know that from my work at the museum. It's the poaching they need to stop. Secondly, they're doorstepping in the wrong area. There are no elephants in Little Pride. It's as daft as campaigning to end whale hunting while at the top of Everest.'

'Actually, that would be a great publicity coup,' said Robert with a wry smile. 'Anyone scaling Everest with a model whale would gain plenty of attention for their cause worldwide. But we digress.'

I laughed, glad to have a reason to do so. But my mirth was soon quashed when I remembered the implications of the message.

'Perhaps someone thinks there's ivory in my shop.'

Robert frowned. 'In the chess sets?'

'Presumably.' I nodded towards my window display. 'It's unfortunate that one of them consists of lots of little elephants, but I know they're not ivory. Steven – the friend who I'm selling them for...' I still hadn't told Robert about my failed relationship. No one likes to admit to what would have amounted to divorce, if we'd ever married. 'Steven would never knowingly have bought ivory. In fact, the one time he came to a special African art exhibition at the museum, he gave me a really hard time that some ivory carvings were included, even though they were legacy possessions, rare and unique, kept only in museums, and therefore compliant with the law.'

My eyes widened at the belated thought that this might have been a double bluff on Steven's part, designed to conceal that he'd been illegally acquiring ivory artefacts himself. After all, ivory had once been a coveted, respectable material for prestigious chess sets. But I had no real reason to suspect him of such a dreadful crime. The fact that he was supposedly bound for India, one of only two places in the world that were home to elephants, was pure coincidence.

Conscious that I might be over-reacting to the ketchup message, perhaps spooked by its visual similarity to fresh blood, I slumped back in the chair and tried to gather my thoughts.

'Well, then, your conscience is clear,' said Robert. 'I don't think you should waste another second worrying about it.' His reassuring smile reminded me how neat and white his teeth were.

Now that my pulse had returned to normal, I began to feel a little foolish.

'I suppose no real harm's been done,' I conceded, getting

up from my seat. 'It's just a rather bizarre prank, not a threat to my wellbeing. Sorry to have disturbed you, Robert.'

'It's really no trouble, Alice.'

As Robert got to his feet, I realised what a blessing it was that he was the only one to have witnessed my distress. I hoped no other villagers had seen the lettering before I washed it away. Otherwise the village-rumour machine would switch into overdrive. Before long, word would be all over the village that I'd been arrested for trying to sell stolen goods, for animal cruelty, or even for keeping an elephant in my back garden. Local gossip is more energetic than it is accurate.

It would be awful at this stage if some silly misinformation about the nature of my chess sets scuppered our Chessmates launch. An image of Tilly popped into my head. Though a bit young for chess, she had been so keen to support my event. Then Herbie Studge sprang to mind – cheery, chatty Herbie, who I really hoped to introduce to a new passion to trump his interest in gruesome online games.

I wasn't about to let down Tilly, Herbie or any of the village children over a silly practical joke. I marched back into my shop, determined to make the event a resounding success, for their sakes, as much as to restore Steven's solvency.

13

A TESTING TIME

Danny guffawed when I told him about my phantom ketchup artist, then tried to turn his laugh into a cough so as not to offend me.

'I'm sorry you had such a fright,' he said. 'What a stupid prank. Whoever did it must have done so after I'd left for work. I'm sure it wasn't there when I went out this morning. From what you say, I'd have seen it.'

'If not, you'd have skidded on the ketchup.' I laughed, starting to see the funny side myself now.

'I don't think you need worry that it was some kind of professional job, given the medium of the message. But if you're worried about whether any of Steven's chess sets actually are ivory, there's an easy way to tell, even without assuming receipts and letters of provenance that he kept are accurate.'

'Really?' That cheered me up. It was useful to have a fellow museum expert as my lodger, with different specialisms from mine. 'How?'

'Easy-peasy,' said Danny. 'We just heat a fine sewing needle to red hot, then press the point against anything that looks like ivory. If it is ivory, the point won't sink in, but if it's plastic or resin, it will, because the pinprick of heat will melt the material.'

'Are you sure it won't cause any damage? Even though it's illegal to sell ivory, I wouldn't want to be responsible for damaging a rare and valuable artefact.'

Danny shook his head. 'No, it's fine. It's a method that's been used in the antiques trade forever. Come on, get your sewing kit out, and we'll get cracking.'

Working together, we heated needles in a candle flame before touching them against a white piece from each chess set. We probed only the base, so as not to leave a visible mark that might be spotted during play. Thankfully, none of them passed the ivory test.

As a further precaution, we examined every receipt and letter of provenance. Of course, each one was written by a human being, most likely with the best intentions, but fallible all the same. We could not presume these notes were gospel, just the considered judgement of relative experts. Even world-class authorities made mistakes, as I'd learned from reading art historian Brian Sewell's memoirs. The number of fakes believed to be genuine by art dealers was extraordinary.

Experts were rumbled all the time. It would be far easier to fake knowledge as an antique trader than to pass oneself off as, say, a surgeon, where you might daily risk lives. Even so, cases turned up in the media every now and again about fake doctors who had somehow fooled colleagues and patients for years.

Forgers of so many art forms had been uncovered over the

years. Why not a manufacturer of rare chess sets too? With forgers generally operating in isolation, there'd be relatively few experts around to dispute their professional opinion, unlike a fake surgeon, who would be surrounded by medics who might uncover the pretender's secret at any moment during an operation.

'Of course, if we do find any of them are ivory,' said Danny when we were about halfway through, 'you won't be able to sell them at our event.'

'Then what would I do with them?'

'You'd be allowed to keep them for personal use, or you could apply for a licence to sell them to a museum or similar preserver of art and culture. The licence might cost you more than the sale was worth, though, depending on the set's condition.'

I frowned. 'It might also tempt Her Majesty's Revenue and Customs office to throw the book at me. What if they sent government inspectors into my shop and into Steven's storage unit too, to check whether he has any more illegal items tucked away?'

Danny's lips twitched in amusement. 'You don't think that's the real reason Steven fled the country, do you? To escape arrest and imprisonment?'

I snorted with laughter. 'That would explain it. Goodness, I could never be a criminal. I can't even tell white lies.'

Danny grinned. 'Yes, if you tried to flee the country, you'd probably end up confessing and turning yourself in at passport control.'

Sometimes, I think Danny knows me better than Steven ever did.

After putting the last chess set we'd tested back in its box, Danny leaned forward to blow out the beeswax candle, made by a local beekeeper, that we'd used to heat the needles. The honey-scented smoke curled upwards before the wick emitted a last splutter and went out. I watched it fade from brilliant red to dull black.

'OK, duty done,' I declared. 'Now let's get some supper and build up our strength ready for the big day tomorrow.'

14

MATCH DAY

Danny and I arrived at the school hall in plenty of time to set up for the Chessmates launch and sale. The school dinner ladies had helpfully left out the folding tables and stacking chairs the children had used at lunchtime the day before. With the help of Jack Dauntless, Sally Pert and some PTA volunteers, we rearranged some of the tables down one side of the hall to be used to display the more precious sets. We put more tables in a long line in the middle of the room to be used for matches, using the less valuable sets. The set-up reminded me of the vast table at the Mad Hatter's tea party. A dozen little chairs, designed for junior bottoms, were ranged either side of this long line of tables to allow for six games to be played simultaneously. There was also plenty of room for chess coaches and spectators to stand beside the young players and encourage them. Finally, we laid out a few tables and chairs near the serving hatch to be used for teas.

Jack and Sally had thoughtfully mobilised the PTA to organise refreshments. The impressive array of themed cakes on the counter, from checkerboard cookies to gingerbread pawns (essentially limbless gingerbread men), suggested considerable competition between supportive parents, grand-parents and carers.

'We don't do much fundraising here that isn't boosted by sales of tea and cake,' Sally Pert told me as I took a photo-graph of the mouthwatering display.

Danny, Jack and I laid out the chess sets, Jack distributing those robust enough for the children to play with on the central tables. Danny and I, drawing on our museum experi-ence, arranged the more valuable ones artfully on the tables along the side of the hall. I'd prepared a detailed label for every set on sale, outlining its description, age, provenance and price, cribbed from Steven's paperwork.

With the PTA helpers stationed behind the serving hatch, and all the chess sets at the ready, Montgomery Wright emerged from his cupboard-like office at the last minute. I wondered whether he'd been hiding there to avoid having to help us set up, or whether he was just trying to assert his superior status as headmaster. I felt rather sorry for him.

I took up my agreed station by the double doors through which people would enter the hall from the playground, so as to greet people on arrival and explain the layout. On a small side table, I'd put my new card machine, my cash float and a receipt book, ready to take payment for any purchases as buyers departed. This was the only way out of the school at present, all other exits remaining locked.

As people began to arrive, I was gratified to realise how many locals I recognised and who recognised me, either from visiting my shop or from simply passing in the street. It was a village custom to say hello to anyone you met while out walk-ing, whether or not you knew them. In the small community of Little Pride, it's very easy to spot an outsider.

Between them, Jack and Danny had done a great job spreading the word online about the event, while I promoted it locally. I had been hopeful their work would attract people from beyond the parish, as there were only so many chess sets I might hope to sell to locals. There were certainly some strangers in the queue. Even so, soon after the start of the event, I was surprised to see a huge posse of leather-clad motor bikers roar into the small school car park the beyond the playground.

They dismounted and propped the bikes on kickstands. Then, as they crossed the playground, they removed their helmets, revealing beaming, gentle faces and jovial expressions. I gave them a big smile of welcome.

'Hello, love, is Jack Dauntless about, please?' asked the first to approach me, jingling change in his pocket. 'He owes me a rematch.'

'Yes, he's in there supervising the children, but I'm sure he'll be pleased to see you. Perhaps you and he could play a demonstration game for the kids' benefit?'

'That's right, Bishop, let's show the kiddies how it's done,' cried a cheery fellow at the back of the gang.

Bishop? I supposed there was no reason why a bishop shouldn't ride a motorbike. His clerical collar would have been hidden beneath his leather jacket.

'I'm sorry, Your Grace, I didn't realise,' I began, to raucous laughter from his companions.

'No, love, Bishop's his nickname,' said one.

'I'm actually a milkman,' Bishop explained. 'But we all have nicknames, see?'

As one, they turned to show me the backs of their jackets, each bearing a title relating to a chess piece, from Pawno to

Maj, the latter presumably short for His Majesty the King. I took him to be the gang's leader.

They were still chortling good-naturedly as they entered the school hall. Their sudden, noisy arrival made everyone turn and stare. I couldn't help but smile as one small boy took advantage of the distraction to remove one of his opponent's pieces illegally. When he spotted me watching him, he gave me a guilty grin and quickly replaced it.

Jack Dauntless got up from his seat opposite Herbie Studge to stroll over and greet his leather-clad friends, his arms flung wide in welcome.

'Knighty! Rooko!'

In turn they exchanged some sort of fancy handshake with Jack and clapped him on the back. In the hubbub, I missed Jack's moniker, if he had one.

'I'm so glad you guys made it,' Jack was saying as he led them to the display against the far wall. 'There are some cracking sets for sale here. Something to please everyone, I reckon.'

His friends' faces lit up as they gravitated towards the valuable sets. Then the buzz of chatter returned to the hall as normal play was resumed.

Once it seemed as if all the visitors we were likely to get had arrived, Sally Pert kindly offered to take over my station by the double doors. This allowed me to circulate and socialise, and also to get a much-needed cup of tea from the serving hatch. Considering how lightweight the exhibits were, it had been a surprisingly strenuous task to set everything up earlier, and I was feeling dehydrated. The first cup of tea hardly hit the sides, and I took a welcome refill with me as I strolled around the hall to watch the children playing. I hoped none of them would ask my advice on tactics or rules.

By this stage in the event, they probably knew more about the game than I did.

Jack's demonstration match against Bishop, a tall, gaunt fellow with sparse blonde hair and glasses, had drawn a cluster of spectators of all ages, without distracting children engrossed in games of their own. With the wisdom that comes from being a teacher, Jack had imposed a time limit of ten minutes for players to sit at any set. At the tolling of the school's brass handbell, they had to move clockwise to the next seat, reminding me once more of the Mad Hatter's tea party. This ensured no one got stuck in an interminable game, and everyone got a chance to play a few moves against opponents with different ability levels and styles. It also gave as many children as possible the chance to try their hand and familiarise themselves with the board, serving as a great appetiser for the new Chessmates club.

If the club takes off, I thought as I watched one of the older pupils gently advising a younger one on how each piece moved, *my Curiosity Shop might sponsor an annual school chess trophy*. On one of the dressers in my shop stood a trio of silver goblets, part of Nell's old stock. With a bit of silver polish and some strategically placed ribbons, I could easily transform them into desirable trophies. I'd give one for the overall winner of a tournament, another for most sporting player, and the third for most improved or best effort. I could go into school to present it at assembly. I'd been missing the school parties visiting the museum more than I'd expected. Establishing a closer link with the village school would help fill that void.

Just as I was returning to my post by the double doors, clutching a gingerbread pawn and a coffee (always so much tastier when someone else makes it for you), a straggler from the bikers' gang appeared at the entrance, still wearing his helmet.

As Mr Wright tolled the handbell to mark the end of the next ten-minute period, I welcomed the new arrival and explained the set-up. I expected him to go and join his mates, who were now making buying signals, encouraged by the attentions of the lovely Sally Pert. She was gently picking up pieces and holding them up to the light for the bikers to examine more closely. I wondered whether she'd had a former career in sales.

Instead, the newcomer made a beeline to an empty seat just vacated by Herbie Studge. To my delight, Herbie was protesting to his mum that he didn't want to leave to go to his swimming lesson. He wanted to stay here to play chess. The game seemed to have captured his imagination. Perhaps to Herbie, chess seemed as real a battle between opposing forces as any game on his phone, the little horses snickering and the pawns sounding battle cries as they advanced.

'Don't worry, Herbie,' I told him as he said a slightly grumpy goodbye to me on his way out. 'There'll be plenty more opportunities for you to play chess after half term, when Mr Dauntless and Danny – Mr Kimani – will be starting your new school chess club.'

Herbie tugged at his mum's coat sleeve. 'Can I get a set of my own to practise with at home, Mum? Can I have one for my eleventh birthday?'

His mum looked at me with eyes sparkling in surprised delight.

'Grandpa already has one, love. I'm sure he'd love to play with you. He was school champion when he was a boy.'

As Herbie's chest swelled with vicarious pride, a twinge of pain shot through me. If our last attempt at IVF had been successful, Mum would have had a grandchild of Herbie's age now.

Taking a deep breath to distract myself from that thought, I turned my attention to the other players to see who was paired with who after the latest change of seats. To my amusement, the new biker, his helmet now on his lap, had taken a seat opposite Tilly, dwarfed by his bulk. Scowling at the board between them in deep concentration, her hand hovered over one of the chunky Isle of Lewis pawns. I hoped the biker would let her win.

Just then, another latecomer arrived: Robert.

'Sorry not to be here from the start to support you, Alice,' he said, without looking me in the eye. 'I mean, to support the school. My daughter was going to bring Tilly. Are they here already?'

He polled the room until his gaze alighted on an expensively dressed woman with long, honey-coloured mermaid waves. I recognised his daughter, Belinda, from a family photo I'd seen in his entrance hall. When she nodded at him in recognition, he blew her a kiss, and she gave a regal wave before strolling over to join us.

'Hello, Pa,' said Belinda, kissing him on both cheeks. She raised her coffee cup to him. 'Look, I'm slumming it today. I'd usually be having my go-to breakfast of bulletproof coffee about now.' She nodded at the wall clock, which showed midday. 'The start of my window, as you know.' Catching my blank look, she added, 'I do the 18:6, you know.'

Ah, so she was a practitioner of restricted eating. That was completely off my radar. I didn't know what to say about it. So, I resorted to stating the obvious with a conciliatory smile.

'Hello, you must be Belinda,' I said. 'I'm Alice. I live next door to your father.'

She must have known that already, following the events of the summer. Surely Robert must have mentioned me to her, but I didn't want to appear presumptuous.

Robert pulled a handful of coins from his pocket. 'Belinda, darling, be a love and go and get me a normal coffee, would you, while I have a look around? Alice, would you like one too?'

Although grateful for being included, I raised my still half-full cup. 'No thanks, this is my third hot drink since I arrived, so I'm fully caffeinated for now. I recommend the gingerbread pawns, Belinda.'

But she'd already sashayed back across the hall to the serving hatch, bony, boyish hips swinging, without waiting for my answer.

'Bulletproof coffee! Ugh!' Robert grimaced at the mere thought of it.

'I've heard of bulletproof coffee, but I've never tried it. Isn't it just black coffee with fat in it, to fill you up and suppress your appetite?'

'A lump of butter and a slug of oil, I believe. Which is how to ruin a perfectly good cup of coffee, if you ask me.'

'It's not my cup of tea either, if you'll excuse the pun,' I replied, glad to be having a relaxed conversation after our awkward one on the tea terrace the previous day.

Robert had already moved on.

'My word, have you seen who Tilly is playing?' said Robert, nodding towards the latecomer biker, who was currently taking one of her pawns. Her side, the whites, looked much reduced compared to her opponent's. 'I don't suppose that will go down well with her. You'd think a big bloke like that would have the decency to let her win.' He tutted in disapproval. 'Anyway, show me around the sets you have on display. Maybe I could treat Tilly to one to encourage her to take up chess. She's a bright little thing, and she's naturally a strategic thinker.'

I led Robert to the sets displayed at the side of the hall. Belinda brought him his coffee, then went to sit with some other mums at one of the tea tables. I was disappointed not to have the chance to befriend her a little, for Robert's sake. Not that I was thinking of her as a possible future daughter-in-law, or even a near neighbour, closeted as she was over in snooty Great Pride. From the designer labels on her leisurewear and her wristwatch, I guessed she was never going to be a customer of my Curiosity Shop either. Oh well, as long as her choices made her happy, who was I to criticise? Except she didn't seem exactly happy just now.

When Robert went to get a refill and sit with his daughter, I decided it would be politic to stroll around the players' tables to see how everyone was getting on. More adults had joined in as children lost interest – or succumbed to the pull of the cake display – cramming their grown-up-sized bottoms onto the small children's chairs. At a couple of playing stations, a few little ones were making up their own games, treating the chess pieces as tiny dolls, like Playmobil or Lego figures.

'I'm just taking my horsey to visit that castle over there,' one earnest little boy in round, wire-rimmed glasses was explaining to his friend.

In his chubby hand, a white knight hopscotched across the board, pushing a white castle slightly to one side so that they could share the same square.

Some of Jack's biker friends had also settled down to play, a few of them in league with small children, turning the games into doubles matches and whispering advice behind their hands to their young companions. It was heartwarming to see Steven's chess sets being deployed to enrich the local community, bringing children and adults of all ages closer together in a way that hadn't been available to them before.

As I returned to my seat by the door, facing the playground with my back to the school hall, I was glad to realise all the sounds in the room were happy – the high-pitched chatter of excited small children, the tinkling of coffee cups, the benign hiss of the tea urn. I hoped whoever had ketchuped my patio wasn't in the room. I didn't want anyone upsetting the children or spoiling our event with any more gruesome stunts.

I turned round to check how sales were going. To my delight, I spotted several gaps on the tables displaying the pricier sets. Seeing the first buyer head for the double doors, I returned to my station to take their payment.

'I'd better just check all the pieces are there before I take your money,' I said to a dark, slim man in cycling gear who had chosen the set of Incas and Conquistadors.

While I checked the contents of its box, he regaled me with how he'd wanted to buy a set like this on his recent cycling tour of South America but couldn't justify the pannier space. I decided to make a note of any little anecdotes like this, alongside the buyer's contact details I was writing on my receipts duplicate book, so that I could pass them on to Steven. Knowing the sets had gone to good homes might make him feel less bereft at having to part with them. For all his talk about pursuing a minimalist lifestyle in future, if he'd been sure of that intention in the first place, he would have sold all his collections before he departed. That would have saved him a fortune in storage fees.

The time I spent checking each set as it was sold,

providing the right paperwork and processing payment caused quite a queue to form by the doors. After the last customer had paid, I realised there were only a couple of the fancy sets left on display. I had no idea chess would be so popular in Little Pride. Jack and Danny had clearly done a brilliant job attracting serious buyers, not just curious observers.

Flicking through the receipts book, I calculated that I'd taken nearly two thousand pounds, mostly paid by cards tapped against my phone app, with just one buyer using cash.

Satisfied, I sat back and surveyed the scene. The families were starting to drift away now. They probably all had plenty of other things to do with their Saturdays. But a few stragglers carried on playing, mostly Jack's biker friends, some of whom had already paid me for purchases. One of them was now engaged in a match with Montgomery Wright. The headmaster's pale cheeks were flushed, his eyes glinting. I was glad for his sake that the event seemed to have been a success from the school's point of view as well as my own.

Danny was walking towards me, smiling broadly.

'We've twenty-three takers for the Chessmates club already,' he told me. 'Jack's really pleased, and I've had fun too.'

I paused to thank a departing biker for coming, even though he hadn't bought anything. I couldn't tell which one he was because he'd already replaced his helmet, and there was no name on the back of his jacket, just a geometric pattern in silver studs.

'Didn't see a set that took your fancy?' I queried lightly, trying to sound interested rather than accusatory.

'None that were for sale,' he mumbled, brushing past me.

I hoped I hadn't embarrassed him. Maybe he just hadn't found any that he could afford.

'Anyway, how are sales going?' Danny continued.

Before I could tell him the good news, there was a shrill squeal from the centre of the room, where Tilly had leaped to her feet and was thumping the table with her small, tight fist, making the few pieces left on the board leap about like jumping beans.

'That man cheated me!' she cried, standing up and putting her hands on her hips. 'I've just tried to set the board up for a new game, but most of my side aren't there. I think he stole them.'

She waved at the depleted white ranks of the chunky, plastic Isle of Lewis reproduction set, now outnumbered by their charcoal-grey opponents.

Robert dashed to her side to calm her down. 'I expect they've just fallen under the table. Here, let Grandpa help you find them.'

He beckoned to her to check the floor on her side, as he did on his. After a moment of scrabbling on the floor, they emerged, bearing a few half-eaten biscuits and a small cuddly toy lion, but no chess pieces.

'Well, let's line up what we've got,' said Robert in a conciliatory tone. 'Once they're all on the right squares, you might find there aren't really any missing after all.'

Tilly frowned but sat down and set to work. Robert did the same, looking like a giant on the tiny plastic chair. After a few minutes, she sat back, folded her arms, and huffed. 'I told you so. Sixteen blacks but only five whites, and those are all the little ones – the prawns.'

In an unusual show of anger, she snatched at the pieces with her small fists, sending the neat array of chessmen tumbling all over the place, before thrusting her hands in her dress pockets.

By this time, Belinda had come to see what had upset her daughter.

'I tell you what, Tilly,' said Robert. 'Why you don't you leave me to put what's left of this set away, because it'll be no good for anyone else to play with now. You and Mummy go and have a look at the sets for sale. You don't want an incomplete one like this, but I was thinking of buying a pretty set for you to play with me at my house. You can choose which one.'

Tilly brightened and leaped to her feet, slipping her hand into Belinda's.

I turned to Robert. 'I expect some of the little ones have borrowed some of these pieces to play with and mixed them up with other sets. I don't blame them. The Isle of Lewis chessmen do look a bit like the Vikings' answer to Weebles.'

'I'm sorry if it was Tilly,' said Robert, pulling his wallet from his pocket. 'If you'd care to let me know the set's value, I'll gladly compensate you.'

I waved away his handout. 'Don't worry, it's only a cheap plastic imitation. The other pieces will turn up elsewhere when we gather up all the playing sets.'

A couple of seats further along, a girl of about seven was in the middle of lining up a row of eight knights on one board, clearly pilfered from different sets about the table.

Looking reluctant to abandon his own game against one of the bikers, Mr Wright got up and came to join us, perhaps conscious that he had prioritised his enthusiasm for the game over his responsibilities as headmaster.

'Everything OK?' he asked in a tone that sought only one answer. 'I suppose we had better start to pack up.' He looked at his watch. 'We'd be stretching the goodwill of the PTA to ask them to put in any more time today, much as I'd like to play on.' He glanced back at his unfinished game. 'I'd stay and play all day if it was down to me.'

He stared glumly at the floor for a moment, making me wonder whether he had a welcoming home to go to, or whether his work was his entire life. Then he gave a signal to one of the team behind the serving hatch.

'Half price on all remaining cakes,' she yelled, with the projection and authority of a primary-school teacher.

As one, the remaining bikers swarmed towards the cake stall like shiny black stag beetles to snap up foil-wrapped packages of unsold goodies to take away.

Jack and Danny cleared the chess sets from the central tables while I went to put the remaining fancy ones back in their boxes. Then Tilly came to show me which one she'd chosen for Robert to buy.

'Oh, the Alice in Wonderland one!' I exclaimed, as Robert pulled out his credit card.

Tilly, her usual sunny nature restored by her grandfather's treat, beamed at me.

'Yes, and did you know it's got you in it?' she replied. 'I thought you might like to play chess at Grandpa's house too sometimes.'

The thought of the chess set Steven bought me as a make-up gift now residing at Robert's house made me feel a little uneasy. *Not that Robert is Steven's rival or successor*, I told myself, but the unexpected connection between the two of them made me uncomfortable.

But not half as uncomfortable as the shock that awaited me in the school car park.

15

CHECKMATE

Leaving Mr Wright to lock the school building and set the burglar alarm, Danny, Jack and I headed outside, carrying the remaining sets between us. Jack had kindly offered to run us back to the Curiosity Shop to save me having to fetch my car to collect the remaining chess sets. Spotting a notice on the wall of the school car park prohibiting vehicles other than those belonging to school staff, I'd dropped the chess sets off earlier in the day and driven my car home again. I'd walked back up ready for the start of the event.

'I'm glad I'm not the only one who hasn't got the head-space for chess,' I said as we crossed the playground. 'Did you see those two mums playing draughts on the set nearest the serving hatch?'

Jack laughed. 'Well, why not? As long as they were having fun.'

'You're right. I'm just pleased all these sets were at last being used for games of any kind, after being kept packed away in storage for so long.'

'And the commission you're kindly paying to the school

should buy quite a few sets for the kids to use at our Chessmates club,' said Jack. 'That's brilliant.'

'It was worth all the work in setting the event up,' said Danny.

'My biker friends enjoyed it too,' said Jack. 'It was the first time I'd met some of them in real life. I know them from an internet chess group that I belong to.'

'I recognised a few faces from there too,' said Danny.

'Thanks for luring them along, and others from beyond the school community,' I said to Jack. 'I'm sure we wouldn't have made nearly as much money had we relied on villagers.'

All of a sudden, Danny stopped in his tracks and laid his free hand on my arm.

'Speaking of appearances,' he began. 'This is probably not what it looks like, but I just want to make sure. Stay here with Jack, Alice. Let me just check this out a moment.'

He added the chess sets he was carrying to Jack's pile, then broke into a sprint, stopping only when he reached Jack's small blue camper van in the middle of the school car park. There he crouched down with his back to us, before turning his head to shout across the playground, 'Alice, call an ambulance, quickly. And ask for the police too. One of the bikers has been attacked.'

Then Jack added his stack of chess sets to mine, leaving me standing stock still, with a towering pile in my outstretched arms. I didn't dare move for fear of dropping the lot. I was glad of the excuse to delay encountering what sounded like very bad news.

'Which of them is it?' cried Jack. 'And where are the others? Why didn't they stop and help?'

After carefully putting all the chess sets down on the ground, I pulled out my phone and dialled 999. Before I could answer all the call-handler's questions, I had to edge closer to the incident. Wincing at the biker's head injury, I realised the injured person on the ground was not one of Jack's online friends, but the latecomer without a nickname on his jacket.

By now, Jack was kneeling beside the sprawled body, two fingers on the casualty's neck. He closed his eyes and shook his head before gazing mournfully at me.

'I think the ambulance will have a wasted journey, Alice. There's no pulse, and he feels cool to the touch.'

I relayed this information to the call handler.

'I'm afraid we don't know his name or age,' I added. 'But looking at the pool of blood beneath his head, the poor guy hasn't died of natural causes.'

She said she'd send the ambulance anyway, and also the police, as quickly as possible. We were to call straight back if there were any further developments. It hadn't occurred to me until then that the man's attacker might still be lurking nearby.

After ending the call, I glanced nervously around the car park. I was very glad Danny and Jack were with me.

'The motive can't have been theft of his motorbike, as it's still here,' said Jack.

The bike had fallen from its kickstand and lay on its side a metre or so away from its erstwhile rider. The two sturdy panniers lay open, their contents spilled out on the ground. Not that there was much to spill – only a few bits of emergency kit, such as a high-visibility vest, and, pathetically inadequate in the circumstances, a small green zip-up first aid kit.

'And they left his crash helmet,' I added. With my habitual tidiness, I took a step towards the shiny, black helmet that lay beside the bike, unstable on its curved back, planning to set it on its flat base to stop it rolling away. Just in time, I stopped myself from picking it up.

'Oh, my goodness, I think I've found the murder weapon,' I gasped. My throat had tightened in horror at the sight of the blood spattered across the back of the helmet, and I could hardly get the words out.

At Danny and Jack's puzzled looks, I forced myself to elaborate.

'It looks as if someone used the crash helmet as a blunt instrument, bashing him on the head with its hard shell. Goodness, how awful to be killed by the very thing that was meant to protect him. It's like being suffocated by a car airbag.'

From the extent of the damage inflicted, it was easy to see that whatever the helmet was made of was more than a match for the biker's skull.

Was this the byproduct of some kind of biker gang war with Jack's mates, or of intense rivalry in the chess fraternity? I couldn't believe a board game could be so dangerous. Nor could I imagine Jack's friends had been involved. They'd all turned out to be so pleasant.

'I don't think it was a random bit of brutality, though,' said Jack. 'Look, whoever did it went through his pockets after he was out cold.'

From the comfort of Danny's arms, I noticed that the biker's jacket pockets had been turned inside out, and the linings of his trouser pockets were showing too. If the motive was robbery, it was of something small enough to fit in his pockets.

'Or dead,' I murmured. The paramedics' sad task would be to convey him to the local hospital's mortuary rather than the accident and emergency department. I sighed. 'Poor man must be somebody's son. Whoever his mother is, assuming she's still alive – and he looks young enough for that to be the case – I bet she's always been worried about him coming to grief on his motorbike. Although she could never have imagined something like this.'

I gave a choking sob, remembering the times I'd worried about Steven's safety as he commuted to work. I buried my head in Danny's chest.

'We'd better not touch anything as it's a crime scene,' said Danny, as Jack bent over the body. But his warning came too late. In a kindly effort to give the poor fellow as much dignity as might be found in such an awful situation, Jack had stooped to brush the dishevelled, long hair out of the body's wide-open, unseeing eyes. As he did so, he revealed an inscription, left in Sharpie pen, across the stranger's high forehead: *Checkmate.*

It wasn't the blaring siren approaching up the high street that sent a shiver down my spine, but the dawning realisation that my sale of Steven's chess collection was somehow the cause of the poor man's murder.

16

RULED OUT

'Do you think it's got any connection with the anti-ivory campaigner's protest on my doorstep?' I asked Danny once we were back at the Curiosity Shop.

Although Danny had been the one supporting me, all three of us were ashen as we sipped large mugs of sweet tea. Danny and I had collapsed on the sofa. Jack had gone into the back garden to phone Bishop.

We'd piled the remaining chess sets on the shop counter. It was too soon to start sorting them out again, as our innocent plan had been when we left the school hall. We'd not be able to concentrate. Besides, finding the missing pieces from the set Tilly had been playing with and sorting the rest into complete sets seemed very low priority now.

'I can't think how the two things could be related,' Danny replied, sinking back onto the sofa and closing his eyes. 'If someone's going to be upset about ivory poaching, I hardly think they'd have the stomach to bash a human being's head in. Still, I guess we'll know more after the police have finished their investigations. At least they should be able to tell us where the victim came from and what his name is, going by the registration plate of his motorbike.'

Jack came back into the room, tucking his phone into his back pocket. 'Well, I've just spoken to Bishop, and he said they didn't see the solitary biker in the playground when they left, only his bike. I'm not sure they even spoke to him inside the school hall. Bishop said the guy was keeping himself to himself, just looking intently at all the chess sets on display, then he sat down for a token game with Tilly before taking off again.'

'He certainly didn't buy a set to take away with him,' I said, 'so it's not as if he was killed by someone who wanted to steal his purchase. And why kill someone for a chess set anyway? None of them were worth over a hundred pounds – or at least, that's the most Steven paid for any of them. It makes no sense.' I covered my eyes with my hands.

'I suppose the police will want to interview Tilly as well as us,' said Danny. 'And probably everyone else who was at the event. How awful for the kids.'

'I'm sure the police will cause the least upset possible,' said Jack. 'They'll use detectives specially trained to deal with children.'

'Even so, Tilly's mother will never forgive me, and I don't blame her.' I groaned. *Nor*, I thought to myself, *will Robert*. 'Or the rest of the school community. I'll probably get drummed out of Little Pride. Just when I was starting to feel less of an incomer here.'

A sharp rap at the shop door made me look up. Reluctant to receive any customers in my current state of shock, we'd kept the *Closed* sign up on our return.

'I'll get it,' said Danny, getting to his feet.

He returned from the shop a few minutes later after a low

|

exchange of voices. I couldn't make out a word of their conversation, and I didn't really want to.

'It was your next-door neighbour, Robert,' said Danny. 'He'd seen the flashing blue lights heading for the school and wanted to check you were OK. When I told him you were, he went away again.'

Danny sat down on the sofa, resting his elbows on his knees and his head in his hands.

'At least we're all each other's alibi,' he said.

Jack drew in a quick breath, making me look at him with a sudden feeling of doubt. We may all have walked across to the car park together, but might Jack – friend of many bikers – have left the building earlier in the afternoon and done the deed without us noticing? Perhaps when Sally Pert was holding the fort for me at the door? Then I wouldn't have seen him come and go.

'Are there any security cameras in the school grounds, Jack?' I asked, hoping that the car park at least might be under permanent surveillance.

Jack was silent for a moment.

'Yes,' he said at last. 'But they're only on when the whole school security system is turned on. Which it wasn't, because we left Mr Wright switching it on at precisely the time we were crossing the car park. I think we'll all agree that the man must have been dead for a while, as he was cool to the touch. So, there is probably a nice clear shot of us arriving at the crime scene, but no chance of catching the murderer on film.'

I sighed. 'So, I guess it's now in the hands of the police, who will be calling on us all soon to gather evidence.'

At the crime scene, we'd had to give the police our addresses and phone numbers before we were allowed to go home. We left Mr Wright, whose pale face had acquired a green tinge on learning the bad news, giving them access to school files for the contact details of staff and visiting families.

'I expect they'll do door-to-door enquiries through the whole village,' I speculated. 'Anyone passing by the school might have seen important evidence, even if they hadn't attended the Chessmates launch.'

'I bet they ask me to rat on my mates when they discover I'm friends with the other bikers,' said Jack, looking at the floor.

Danny furrowed his brow. 'It's only ratting if they're guilty, Jack.'

Jack gave an apologetic half-smile. 'Yes, of course. I'm sorry to sound so selfish. It's just that the shock of it all is starting to catch up with me.' He got to his feet. 'If you don't mind, I'll head home now. I could do with a bit of time alone to process what's happened.'

As he headed for the door, he paused to lay his hand gently on my shoulder. 'Thanks again for all you've done for the school, Alice, and for inspiring our new chess club. I'm sorry it's turned so nasty. Please don't blame yourself for any of this.'

I didn't reply but sat motionless until Danny had seen Jack out of the shop and locked the front door behind him. There was no way we'd be reopening for the last part of the day.

As Danny returned, I sprang to my feet, raising clenched fists. Danny stepped back in alarm.

'Of course it's not my fault!' I bellowed. 'Of course I'm not going to blame myself that some random attacker takes against a stranger on a motorbike! What does Jack Dauntless take me for? Or was that a double bluff? Was he really suggesting that it is all my fault? For goodness' sake, all I was trying to do was help his wretched school, and to get Steven out of a financial hole of his own making. I didn't want any of this!'

Steven. A horrible new thought occurred to me. Supposing someone had assumed the stranger on the bike was Steven? As the sets we were selling were being offered in Steven's name, which was all over the receipts and provenance papers, someone who didn't know we'd split up or that he'd left the country might have assumed that the lone biker in the car park was him.

But who could Steven have enraged so much that they set out to kill him? Could it have anything to do with the gambling debts he'd incurred on his travels? I pictured a ruthless, Mafia-style pursuer stalking him, planning to punish him for non-payment.

I threw myself back on the sofa.

'Whatever Jack Dauntless thinks, whatever Belinda, or Robert, or Montgomery Wright think, I'm going to find out the truth,' I pledged to Danny. 'There's too much at stake for me to sit idly by while the police start their investigation from scratch. There have to be some clues out there that we just haven't yet recognised as such. For the sake of the school, of my shop, and my village life, I'm going to do my very best to find them.'

17

MISSING PIECES

'Did you notice Jack Dauntless has a World Wide Fund for Nature bumper sticker on his camper van?' I asked Danny mid-morning on Sunday. After forcing down a breakfast of toast and local jam that neither of us felt very hungry for, we were once more spreading out chess sets on the shop counter to check their contents. Secretly, I hoped setting them all up again might jog my memory about some vital but forgotten detail of the previous day's drama.

'So do a lot of people, but it doesn't mean they go around bumping off bikers,' replied Danny evenly. 'I think you're barking up the wrong tree if you think Jack Dauntless is the villain in all this.'

'Just because he's got a name like a comic book hero...'

'And the physique of one,' murmured Danny.

I hoped he wasn't going to allow his new friendship with Jack to cloud his judgement.

'That doesn't mean we can let him off the hook either,' I retorted. 'Especially when our hook is otherwise empty.'

'Then perhaps we need to add some bait,' said Danny.

I rolled my eyes. 'What is this, National Cliché Day?'

Danny slumped back in his chair. 'Come on, Alice, cut me a little slack. The last twenty-four hours have been extremely stressful for both of us, but let's be rational here. We need to think the whole event through carefully and take our time. But first, let's get these remaining chess sets sorted and put away, and clear the counter ready for you to open the shop as usual tomorrow. You've lost the whole weekend's trading, and you mustn't let this awful situation disrupt your business just when the shop is really starting to take off.'

I closed my eyes and drew a few deep breaths. 'Yes, you're right, Danny. I'm sorry. And thank you, as ever, for looking after me in a time of crisis. I don't know what I'd have done without you if you hadn't been here yesterday. I certainly wouldn't have wanted to spend the night here alone.'

A mischievous twinkle came into Danny's dark eyes. 'There's always the boy next door to call on.'

I found myself wishing that were true. Although after involving poor little Tilly in the murder victim's final game of chess, it seemed unlikely Robert would ever want anything to do with me again. That was probably why he'd called round the previous evening – to complain vehemently on behalf of his precious granddaughter and her mother. No wonder Danny had prevented him from seeing me. He did the right thing. Being admonished by a justly furious Robert would have tipped me over the edge of reason.

We set to work.

* * *

About an hour later, I closed the last box, all the remaining chess sets checked and accounted for. Thankfully, almost all were complete. I'd been worried that the children, anthropomorphising the pieces, might have been tempted to slip them into their pockets and smuggle them out. Only the Isle of Lewis set had pieces missing – the set that Tilly and the dead biker had been playing with.

'Poor Tilly. No wonder she was uncharacteristically stroppy. She's usually a chirpy little soul. She was just expressing righteous indignation. But why would the biker steal relatively worthless chess pieces? It's not as if they're the real ones pinched from the British Museum. It's just a plastic reproduction set. You can buy new ones for about twenty quid. We did test that set for ivory, didn't we?'

Danny nodded. 'Yes, of course. I tested the white king, and I distinctly recall thinking that his bulbous eyes made him look as if the needle had actually hurt him.'

I opened the box again to look at Steven's receipt.

'Steven only paid thirty quid for it in the first place,' I said.

'And even if the biker was planning to resell them – I suppose he might have been a drug addict, desperate to earn any money he could to pay for his next fix – surely, he must have realised a partial set would have no value at all? It would make more sense if he'd pinched a complete set.'

I considered for a moment. 'Perhaps he was aiming to steal the whole set, but someone spotted what he was up to, making him flee before he was done. He did leave rather abruptly.'

'What a pathetic petty crime to pull in a school environment in the presence of kids. Anyone who did seem him pocketing pieces, like Tilly, would have been justifiably angry. But sufficiently incensed to follow him out to the car park and kill him there? I don't think so. Some of those PTA ladies looked a bit fierce, and I wouldn't like to get on the wrong side of Miss Boulder, but they're hardly murderous types.'

I piled up the boxes against the wall at the far end of the counter, leaving space clear for serving customers when I re-opened the shop. I'd already decided it would be disre-spectful to the dead man to open on Sunday, and now decided to keep it closed on Monday too. I needed a little more time to process what had happened before I was ready to welcome customers with my usual friendly smile.

We wandered back into the kitchen to wash our hands at the sink, conscious that many people must have handled the chess pieces earlier, including numerous schoolchildren. We didn't want to pick up any autumn-term germs.

Returning to the sitting room with fresh cups of coffee, Danny made himself comfortable on the sofa, his stockinged feet on the coffee table, while I set a fire in the wood burner. Before long, we had the much-needed comfort of a roaring flame to gaze at through the stove's little windows.

But the moment I sat down on the armchair, I jumped straight up again, splashing coffee down the front of my jeans.

'Hang on!' I cried. 'How come no one discovered his body in the car park before we did?'

Danny reached up to take my mug from me and set it safely on the coffee table before I could spill any more.

'Because none of the staff left before us? It's a staff-only car park, remember. Strictly speaking, the guy shouldn't have parked his bike there. The signs on the gate make that clear enough. Mind you, being murdered is a harsh penalty to pay for parking in the wrong place.'

I let out a bark of laughter. 'You make it sound as if an officious traffic warden had bumped him off. We don't get any traffic wardens around here, because there aren't any yellow lines on the streets of Little Pride.'

Danny shook his head. 'Such a refreshing change from parking in Broadwick, where they'll practically book you for stalling your car if you're not quick off the mark to restart.'

My eyes widened at a sudden recollection. 'But, Danny, he wasn't the only visitor to park in the school car park against the rules. All Jack's biker mates parked there too. In fact, they arrived first and left their bikes there en masse.'

Danny ran his hand across his face in thought. 'And the big group of bikers left the hall long after the murder victim. If he was killed before they left, they'd have seen him lying there and raised the alarm. He might even still have been alive at that point.'

We locked eyes for a moment as another theory dawned on us simultaneously.

'Unless...' I hesitated, not wanting to declare what we were both thinking.

Danny finished my sentence for me. 'Unless he was still alive when they went out to the car park, and they killed him before speeding away.'

'But not before raiding his pockets and panniers for whatever contraband was stowed there.'

'Drugs, do you suppose?' mused Danny. 'Are the missing chess pieces a red herring? A cover story for a drug dealer?'

'Only if the stolen chess pieces had still been in his pockets when he was left for dead. Which they weren't, not as far as I could see anyway. I suppose they could have been in hidden pockets or perhaps the sort of body belt that some people use abroad to protect their passports and foreign currency from pickpockets.'

'Do you suppose we should tell the police about the missing chess pieces? We can say that if they found any on the dead man, they should be restored to their rightful owner. Which is true. If the police have them, they should give them back to you for Steven.'

I grimaced. 'If they were in secret pockets, the police will probably want to keep them as evidence, at least for now. They may well be fingerprinting them as we speak.'

'And finding Tilly's little paws have been all over them.'

'Don't, Danny, please! Yesterday has probably scarred her for life without you citing her as a possible murder suspect.'

Not to mention the risk of alienating her grandfather forever – and her mother, Belinda.

'I suppose the best thing to do would be to raise the matter when the police come to interview us,' said Danny. 'It would be the least disruptive to the proceedings and save drawing too much attention to ourselves. Not that we've anything to hide, of course.'

As if sensing my discomfort, he came over to kneel by my chair and laid his arm around my shoulders.

'Have faith in the police, Alice. I'm sure everything will be OK in the end. And at least you're helping Steven solve his problem.'

'Ah, yes, Steven.' I sighed and rested my head on Danny's shoulder. Could there really be a chance that Steven was somehow mixed up in all this too?

Danny laid a reassuring hand on my knee. 'Anyway, as you said earlier, we can help move things along by conducting our own investigation.'

'We?'

'Naturally, you can count on me to help you wherever I can.'

When I shuddered, Danny pulled me closer to him – a kind and comforting gesture that made me think for a moment that perhaps things weren't quite as bad as they seemed.

Until my mother walked in.

18

ENTER THE RED QUEEN

'Alice Carroll, what on earth is going on?'

'Mum!' I squealed in surprise.

Danny and I jumped apart so quickly that an uninformed observer might have thought we had guilty consciences. As did my mother.

'Danny, this is my mum, Wendy,' I said quickly. 'Mum, this is Danny.'

She set her suitcase beside the empty armchair opposite me and threw herself down into it without even taking off her coat.

'Alice, why ever haven't you told me about your new man?' She narrowed her eyes at him. 'Or is Danny the real reason that you and Steven split up?'

Danny leaped to his feet and took a few paces back. 'I'm sorry, Mrs Carroll, but Alice has had a nasty shock, and I was just comforting her as a friend.'

Mum looked his broad-shouldered figure up and down, not unappreciatively. I closed my eyes, hoping she wasn't about to change her tune and suggest he'd make a fitting replacement for my ex. She'd never given up on the hope of marrying me off, whether to Steven or anyone else. Perhaps it was a tribute to the strength of her relationship with my dad that she didn't seem to understand that it was possible to be happy without being married.

'Danny used to work at the museum with me, Mum,' I explained, smoothing my hair. I was aware I might have been looking a bit dishevelled. That wasn't helping my argument.

'I see.' She narrowed her eyes. 'And where do you work now, Danny?'

Danny edged towards the sofa and sat down on the end furthest from Mum. 'Still at the museum.'

Mum flashed me a quizzical look, and I groaned.

'Sorry, Mum, I hadn't got round to telling you. I don't work there any longer.'

She raised her eyebrows at me.

'So where do you work, dear?' She jabbed a thumb behind her in the direction of the shop. 'Don't tell me you've become a shopkeeper. I thought this was just what the old lady who died here had left behind when you bought it.'

When I gave a slight nod, she clapped one hand over her bifocals.

'Alice, when you sent me your change of address card, you said you were moving into an old shop to turn it into a home. You didn't mention anything about swapping your career as a cultural educator to run a junk shop. Otherwise, what is the point of your history degree?'

That old chestnut! Mum tended to dress up my job at the museum with a range of fancy titles of her own devising, as much to impress herself as anyone else. She had always been disappointed that, after being the first in our family to go to university, I hadn't gone into one of the traditional professions such as accountancy or law. I'd long ago given up trying to persuade her that I was doing far more good by working in a museum than by becoming a wage slave in a boring office.

I sat up a little straighter, feeling defensive of the shop that I'd worked so hard to revive.

'Actually, Mum, I consider the shop a natural successor to the museum. I'm drawing on so much of my experience and training – identifying and valuing vintage things; preserving and displaying them imaginatively and appealingly; and running the administrative side efficiently.'

Mum blinked a few times before leaning back and letting out a deep sigh of relief. 'Oh, so it's an antiques shop, rather than a junk shop? Something high quality? Well, why didn't you say?'

I shook my head in silent despair.

'What's more,' put in Danny, coming to my rescue as ever, 'she's becoming a mainstay of the village community. She's now editor of the *Little Pride Parish News* and a valued supporter of the village primary school. We've just been up there this weekend. Alice has been launching a chess club for the children's benefit.'

Mum turned her piercing blue eyes on me. 'But you don't play chess. When Steven bought you that beautiful Alice in Wonderland set, you complained to me what a thoughtless gift it was, even though you knew what a huge fan I am of Lewis Carroll.'

'It would have been thoughtful if he'd bought it for you, Mum,' I retorted. 'But it was just an excuse for him to buy yet another chess set for his collection. It was never really for me.

But he's changed his mind about it now, because he's commissioned me to sell his whole chess collection for him, including that Alice in Wonderland set.'

I hadn't meant to tell Mum about Steven's straitened circumstances, and I was relieved she didn't grill me further.

'Well, I'd be happy to take the Alice set off your hands. You know I've always coveted it. How much is he selling it for?'

'I'm sorry, Mum, I'm afraid it's too late. I sold it to someone else yesterday.'

Before she could object, I changed the subject. It was bizarre how we'd got into a debate about my love life and my career without any explanation for her sudden appearance or even a hello.

'Anyway, what are you doing here? I wasn't expecting you. Hello and welcome, by the way.' I got up to give her a gentle kiss on the cheek. I wasn't displeased to see her, but her sudden appearance was a shock to my already jangling nerves.

She reached up to wrap her arms around me in a stiff hug. When she released me, I noticed Danny looking relieved. I'd never had cause to tell him that my relationship with my parents, who were often critical of my life choices, was somewhat robust – a necessary attitude to keep us close while agreeing to disagree. My mum was the polar opposite of Danny's mother, whom I'd met several times. Danny's mum was warm, tactile, uncritical and unquestioningly supportive of whatever he did, and they never argued. Perhaps that was why Danny was such a teddy bear of a friend.

'Well, you did say I'd be welcome any time, dear,' she reproached me.

'Yes, but a bit of warning – I mean, advance notice –

would have been helpful. You could easily have texted me. Otherwise, you might have come all this way only to find I'd gone on holiday.'

That image sounded very appealing right now, even though living in a tiny Cotswold community surrounded by beautiful countryside was in many ways like being on permanent vacation.

'But I did,' she objected.

She picked up her handbag, in the style favoured by the late Queen, and unclipped the gilt clasp. After pulling out a small, basic mobile phone, she removed it from its pink and white crocheted cover. It was from Mum that I learned all my needlework skills, although my projects look rather different from hers. She tapped a couple of buttons and passed the phone to me to read.

'Arvg Sat 2pm 4 1 wk LOL,' I read aloud. 'Mum, you do know text messages no longer restrict you to a limited number of characters? You can just type in the same kind of language that you'd use to speak to me. It won't cost you any more money. And LOL? Is that a typo? What did you mean to say?'

'Why, lots of love, of course.'

I pressed my lips together to disguise a smile. 'Anyway, you haven't pressed send.'

When I handed the phone back to her, she immediately clicked the send button, making my phone on the coffee table emit a quick burst of 'Mamma Mia', the alert sound I'd set specifically for her communications. Although I can access the local mobile signal for calls only in my garden, somehow, text messages always manage to penetrate the thick walls of the Curiosity Shop.

'There you are. Now, you said you've got a spare bedroom, and I'm welcome to stay any time.'

That was true. I had offered her an open invitation when I sent the change of address card. I hadn't anticipated her turning up at a tricky moment like this. All the same, she was here now, and I knew I should make the best of it.

'I have, but I'm afraid it's Danny's room just now,' I replied.

Mum always did have terrible timing.

'Oh.' She looked from one of us to the other. 'So, you're not... or is this the modern way for partners now, to sleep in separate rooms? All this nonsense about people needing their own space. Me and your father never did. If me-time was that crucial, they'd have put it in the wedding vows.'

So, the first overt mention of marriage. I wondered how many more she'd notch up before she left.

'Mum, Danny's my lodger,' I explained. 'I'm just putting him up in my spare room for a while because he's between flats in the city. But don't worry, you can have my room. That spare room's nowhere near as nice, anyway. My bedroom's the only room I've had a chance to decorate so far in the accommodation part of the property.'

It was true. I'd had fun applying the cottagecore look to my bedroom using bits and pieces from my shop. She was bound to like it.

'I can easily sleep on the sofa down here,' I added. 'It pulls out into a comfy bed. I really don't mind.'

Mum's features relaxed a little. 'Well, if you're sure you don't mind, dear, that would be lovely. If you show me where it is, I'll go up and unpack, and then you can tell me all about your little chess event at the village school over a nice supper.

Then we can sit by the fire and do our knitting together. It'll be just like old times.'

She got up and headed for the stairs, leaving me to carry her suitcase.

'Apart from the tall, dark, handsome lodger,' I whispered to Danny, grinning, before following her out of the room.

19

COLLABORATION

'She's like Miss Marple, knitting away in there,' said Danny in a low voice, prodding a wooden spoon into the bubbling pan of pasta. 'Does she have the same talent for deduction? She may well come in handy.'

I sprinkled chopped onion across a film of sizzling oil in the frying pan. 'I think you'll find Miss Marple knitted for the pleasure of it, rather than because it triggered some kind of detective superpower. She had endless nieces and nephews to knit for. Plus, it disguised her intelligence. Agatha Christie thought no one would suspect an apparently harmless old biddy knitting away as capable of observation or intellectual thought. But we know that's not true, don't we?'

Danny grinned as I passed him a jar of passata to open.

'So, when are you going to tell her about the murder?' he queried, his smile fading. 'And how?'

'Which one?' I said, realising I hadn't told her about the whole awful business from the summer yet either. I clapped my hands over my mouth and burst out laughing. 'Goodness, just listen to me! Which one, indeed! Danny, has moving to the countryside made me callous? When I lived in Broadwick, the sight of a dead pigeon on the street would reduce me to tears. Now I've got dead people turning up on my doorstep, and I appear to be taking it in my stride.'

'It's called gallows humour,' Danny reminded me. 'It's just a coping mechanism. And don't be too hard on yourself. You're still in shock. Don't think I didn't notice you cut your finger when you were chopping herbs just now, because your hands were shaking so much. You need to take it easy for the next few days while you get over it – and to brace yourself for whatever the police investigation throws up. It's not going to be much fun.'

He was right, of course.

'Actually, I told Mum about yesterday's crime while I had her on my own upstairs just now, so that's one thing less to worry about. But what do we do now? Mum's sudden appearance, like she'd just teleported herself down from the Starship *Enterprise*, has put me right off my stride.'

'How did she get in, by the way? Had you sent her a door key in the post?'

I shook my head. 'I must have left the shop door unlocked after I put the bins out earlier. Easily done. Although if she's staying for more than a day or two, I'd better get a spare key cut for her.'

'I'll get one done for her when I go to work tomorrow,' said Danny, setting the old cream and green enamel colander over the sink ready for draining the pasta. 'I'm glad she's come just now, because otherwise, I'd have been reluctant to leave you here on your own on Monday.'

'That's very kind of you, but I'm sure I'll be fine, with or without Mum. Although now that I think about it, I'm glad to have Mum here for her distraction value. I bet she'll get overexcited when I show her Maudie's button box.'

'Why don't you do that now, and I'll finish cooking supper?' Danny suggested. 'It'll give her something nice to take her mind off the news you've just told her about the murder.'

How did such a caring man as Danny end up with lowlife like Martin? He really deserved so much better. I stood on tiptoe to give him a chaste kiss on the cheek.

'Thanks, Danny, you're a pal.'

He grinned. 'No problem. I'd do the same for all my landladies.'

I paused, one hand on the doorhandle. 'I wish we knew the poor guy's name. The way we have to talk about him like some unknown, unloved vagrant seems awfully dehumanising.'

'I daresay we'll know soon enough,' said Danny. 'It'll be all over the news once they've traced his next of kin to get the body formally identified.'

'His poor mother,' I murmured, and headed for the sitting room for some quality time with mine.

20

KNIGHTMARE

Tired after her long drive across the country, Mum went to bed not long after we'd finished our pasta. Her yawns were infectious, making Danny and I realise how weary we were too after the physical, mental and emotional strains of the previous day. After sharing the washing-up, followed by comforting mugs of cocoa by the dwindling fire, I fetched a spare set of bedding from a green Lloyd Loom ottoman before Danny went to bed.

Converting the sofa into a bed, I realised this was the first time anyone had slept on it since I'd moved in. Having two guests in the house made me feel more settled. This truly was my home now, perhaps even my forever home. The gentle crackling of the fire and the rhythmic ticking of the grandfather clock quickly soothed me into the deep sleep of the truly exhausted.

So, when my surprisingly dreamless peace was interrupted by the unmistakeable sound of the shop door clicking open and closing again, I awoke with a start, disoriented. It was a moment before I realised where I was – in the sitting room behind the shop – rather than upstairs in my bedroom – and that at this hour of the night, the shop door should be locked and bolted.

Drat! I thought, dragging myself up into a sitting position. In all the excitement of her unexpected arrival, I'd forgotten to lock the front door. *Taking the day off tomorrow will do me good*, I told myself as I slid my feet into my slippers. *If I have a good lie-in and a restful day, perhaps I'll be thinking a bit straighter when I open the shop on Tuesday and tackle the pile of paperwork necessary following the sale. Plus, I should put the rest of the valuable chess sets on eBay.*

I glanced at the clock, expecting it to be about 3 a.m., but to my surprise, it was only just after 9.30 p.m. We'd all had an early night, going to bed around 9 p.m., drained by the day's events.

As I wandered out into the shop, I was mentally still writing my to-do list. But then in the moonlight filtering through the shop windows, I saw a short fellow in a leather jumpsuit and a motorbike helmet. When he opened one of the chess sets on top of the pile on the counter, I let out a loud gasp, inadvertently alerting him to my presence.

'Excuse me!' Instinctively, I fell into my best assertive, scolding voice that I habitually used for naughty children at the museum who ignored the 'do not touch' labels. 'What do you think you are doing?'

I flicked the light on, blinking against its brightness as I approached the counter. When he did not respond, I felt compelled to fill the silence.

'Isn't it perfectly clear from the time of night and the darkness that my shop is closed? And I'd thank you to take your helmet off before entering the shop as a matter of common courtesy.'

I may have sounded intimidating – or at least I hoped so – but my hands were trembling.

He met my demands halfway by flicking up his visor to reveal grey eyes under bushy eyebrows and a crooked, broken nose made more noticeable by the pressure from the protective framework across his cheekbones.

'It's OK, love, I'm a friend of Nell's,' he said, after glancing at the cash register.

'Nell's never mentioned you to me.'

I followed his line of sight and realised that although I'd had repainted the sign over the shop to say *Alice's Cotswold Curiosity Shop*, I hadn't removed the handwritten sign on the till saying in ornate, cursive, sepia ink, *Welcome to Nell's*.

'It's my shop now,' I persisted. 'And I call the shots.'

No sooner were the words out of my mouth did I realise he might be carrying a gun or other weapon capable of quite a different sort of shot.

The stranger, wearing thick, protective, leather bikers' gloves, ran his forefinger idly over a marble chessboard, tracing the grid lines between the squares.

'Sorry, I never knew that. Haven't been here for a while, you know? Bit of a traveller. An itinerant. A wanderer. Buy and sell antiques wherever I go. Never know where I'll turn up next, or when, from one day to the next. Nell understood, you know? That's why she never minded what hour of day or night I called in. Always knew it would be worth her while to let me in, you know? Always had some sort of little treasure I knew she'd like. Something that would be just right for her old shop.'

'Well, Nell won't be interested where she is now,' I said firmly. 'She's retired. I'm in charge here, and I certainly don't allow anyone to let themselves into my property at any time of night without my prior invitation.'

Now he began to run his finger around the perimeter of the board, perhaps checking for chips or scratches, although I didn't see how he could feel them through those thick gloves. I tried to call his bluff.

'So, what have you brought for her this time? I run the shop now, so if it was something she would have been interested in, I might be too.'

If he didn't produce something, I'd have rumbled him.

I leaned my hands on the counter expectantly.

He gazed at me for a moment, then patted his pockets down as if looking for something and failing to find it. Then he clapped a hand to his forehead.

'Well, what do you know! It must have fallen out of my pocket on the way here. I knew I should have put it in my pannier for safekeeping.' He threw up his hands in mock surrender. 'Hey ho! Well, please give Nell my best. Now I'll be off. Goodnight.'

Before I could challenge what struck me as an obvious lie, he was heading out of the door.

21

LOCKDOWN

By the time I'd locked and bolted the door behind my strange visitor, my heart was racing. I needed a cup of tea to calm my nerves before I'd have any hope of going back to sleep. To my surprise – and relief – Danny was already in the kitchen, putting the kettle on.

'Couldn't you sleep either?' he asked. 'When I came downstairs, I saw you weren't in your bed, then heard you talking to someone out in the shop. I steered clear, assuming it was a late-night romantic tryst with Robert. I didn't like to intrude.'

'No such luck,' I said, before going on to describe my peculiar visitor.

'Are you going to report him to the police?' he asked as we sat on the sofa bed together, nursing mugs of tea.

'Not much point,' I protested, suddenly desperate to sink back into sleep. 'He didn't exactly commit a criminal act. He's probably perfectly innocent. Nell did things her way and made up her own rules, so it wouldn't surprise me if she opened the shop late night occasionally to accommodate out-of-hours deals. Besides, the police will only say it was my silly fault for not locking up. It was rather an open invitation to would-be burglars. I don't think he took anything. Besides, it might invalidate my insurance if it got out that I sometimes forget to lock the shop at night.'

Danny said nothing, just raised his eyebrows at me.

'OK, OK, I promise I'll be more careful in future and be sure to lock and bolt the front door every night.'

'It might also be worth getting a security camera if your budget will run to it,' suggested Danny. 'At least it might have a deterrent effect.'

I closed my eyes, heavy now with exhaustion. 'I've an empty biscuit tin in the kitchen I could paint to look like one. That's what anyone else around here with anything worth stealing does.'

It was true. Theft was virtually unheard of in this place, where everyone knew each other and was swift to notice outsiders behaving suspiciously, at least in waking hours.

'I suppose that would be better than nothing,' said Danny, setting his empty mug on the coffee table and getting to his feet. 'Goodnight, Alice, sleep tight.'

'Night, Danny.'

I snuggled down under the duvet, and almost as soon as he climbed the stairs to his bedroom, I'd drifted off into slumber.

* * *

'You should have shouted to me for help,' Mum declared next morning when I told her about my mysterious visitor over the breakfast table. As she always removed her hearing aids before bed, that probably wouldn't have helped, but I appreciated the thought.

Just as I was finishing my toast, Danny returned from the shop, where he'd been checking the pile of chess sets yet again.

'You'll be dreaming of chess sets at this rate,' I said, secretly thankful that he'd saved me the job.

'The valuable sets are all still intact,' he assured me. 'If last night's intruder took anything, it wasn't a chess set.'

'Value is a subjective thing,' put in Mum. 'The intruder might have been looking to steal something for sentimental reasons. Supposing one of the chess sets had once been owned by the Queen, for example.'

Where did that come from?

'Are intruders usually the sentimental type?' asked Danny, the corners of his mouth twitching in amusement.

'Well, you should know, dears,' Mum retorted. 'You seem to make a habit of fraternising with them around here.'

I'd steeled myself to tell her about the summer murder after supper the night before. I didn't want her to hear it from someone else before me. Although the story had gained Little Pride some coverage in national newspapers at the time, Mum usually got her news input from the WI and her local hairdresser, so I hadn't been particularly worried that she might have read them. Now I realised I should have told her much sooner. I vowed to be a better daughter in future.

'Perhaps you should come back and live with me, dear, as it's clearly not safe around here,' Mum continued. 'I'm rattling around in that big house on my own.'

I wasn't ready to be that good a daughter.

'Or you could take a lodger too, like I have,' I suggested sweetly. 'It would give you extra spending money, and help out a student or nurse, perhaps, in need of affordable accommodation.'

When she looked Danny up and down, he retreated to the kitchen, muttering something about muesli.

'Speaking of Danny,' she continued, 'I think he had better sleep on the sofa tonight, and you take the spare room, just in case your unwelcome visitor returns.'

'I hardly think it likely, Mum. Besides, he only came in because of his arrangement with Nell, and I've put him straight on that.'

Although I didn't want to tell Mum or Danny, the more I thought about it, the surer I was that he'd been lying. A visit to Nell, however, would make it clear.

'Perhaps you'd like to come and visit her with me, Mum,' I suggested. 'Nell said she always welcomes visitors, and I expect she'd be interested to meet you.'

But before I'd had a chance to pursue that idea, my phone rang, and I had to wander out into the back garden in my nightdress and slippers to get enough reception to make out who the caller was, ignoring Mum's cry of, 'But you're still in your nightie! Whatever will the neighbours think?'

'Steven!' I exclaimed as I strolled down the stepping stones to avoid the dew-ridden grass.

'Hi, Alice.'

He sounded cheerier than on his last call. Perhaps it was because he was phoning to find out how much money yesterday's sale had made him. I spared us both the agony of polite, self-conscious small talk and got straight to the point. Well, almost.

'Steven, tell me, are any of your chess sets made of ivory?'

The line crackled. It sounded as if he was in a public call

box, his voice echoey against the distant hubbub of a railway station or airport.

'Ivory? No, of course not. I'm a vegetarian. I'd no more buy an ivory chess set than an elephant's foot umbrella stand.'

I was grateful he'd never collected elephant foot umbrella stands.

'Since when have you been vegetarian?' I didn't want to digress, but Steven had always loved his steaks. Was his Marie Kondo-esque girlfriend to blame for his change of diet? Hats off to them both for making vegetarianism work in France. They must have been living on croissants and *frites*.

'Oh, yes, sorry, I suppose it's only since I've been travelling, but it feels like forever. It's odd, Alice, but time seems to have taken on a different quality lately. The last few months have felt like so many years. In a good way, of course.'

I tried not to take that as criticism of our preceding quarter-century together.

'Anyway, back to your question,' he continued. 'You do know that ivory trading is generally illegal, apart from in very specific circumstances such as museums preserving antiquities. I hope you haven't taken a fancy to it?'

I rolled my eyes. 'Don't mansplain to me about the ivory trade. Have you forgotten my decades at Broadwick Museum? Anyway, the thing is, something odd and rather horrible happened at the sale I organised of your chess sets.'

I explained the incident with the ketchup message, being careful not to mention my shop. For some reason, I wanted to keep that a secret, as part of my new life that wasn't to be shared with him. I rather wished I knew less about his new life too.

'As a lawyer, I've my integrity to think of,' the mansplainer continued. 'If I were caught doing something illegal, my career would be over.'

Not that his integrity as a lawyer really mattered if he was serious about spending the rest of his life travelling the world on his motorbike.

'Anyway, how much money did your sale make for me?' he asked. 'What's the bottom line?'

'What? Oh, sorry, my mind drifted for a moment.'

I had turned to face the high wall between my garden and Robert's. I wondered whether Robert was out of bed yet, breakfasting in silk pyjamas, or maybe nothing but a silk kimono. I looked down at my long, vintage, broderie anglaise nightie, wondering whether he'd think it was frumpy.

Sensing that Steven was starting to lose patience. I spun round to face the empty paddock. There was nothing to distract me there, just the remains of the building site, abandoned after the builder's murder in the summer. Its fate was still unclear.

'About two grand so far, excluding my commission. I'll transfer it into your Wise account tomorrow after I've done the final calculations. The buyers mostly paid online, so it's all safely in my account.'

'You bought a card machine? Was that necessary? You do know you get charged for every transaction on card machines? I hope you're not going to deduct your costs from my proceeds. I'm paying you enough commission as it is.'

'No, we just used our phones,' I improvised. If he knew what a success I was making of the shop, and how much I was enjoying my new lifestyle – apart from the murders, of course – he might feel less guilty about leaving me. I wasn't going to let him off so easily.

I wasn't sure he believed me. Surely after twenty-five years of living together, he ought to have known I was lying, even if he couldn't see me to judge my body language.

I tried to steer the conversation back onto safer ground.

'There are a few sets still to sell that I'm putting on eBay. They were the more valuable ones. I thought I'd put them up for auction and wait to get the best bids online for you, rather than sell them for a fixed price. Now that you've got a couple of grand coming to you to tide you over, I assume you'll be able to wait a bit longer for the proceeds of those sales.'

'Sure, that's great. Thanks, Alice. I really do appreciate your help, you know.'

'So you should,' I retorted, but I didn't say it unkindly. At least he hadn't expected me to bail him out from my own pocket. I was genuinely glad to hear him sounding less anxious.

I took the phone away from my ear for a moment to check which number he was calling from. The country code this time was not the 33 that I knew was France but 39. Italy, I guessed, or Spain, given that they bordered on the south of France.

'Where are you calling from, out of interest?' I asked.

'Why? Does it matter?'

Why was he being so defensive? The question was innocuous enough.

'I just wanted to be able to picture your route. Plot you on my mental map, as if you were Phileas Fogg going around the world in eighty days – or even Michael Palin.'

'OK. Actually, I'm in Sicily. We— I just got off the ferry. I'm in a call box.'

Ah, a ferry terminus was providing the echoey background noise.

'Still no mobile phone, then?'

'No. I didn't bother trying to get one before I left. As I was of no fixed abode and about to leave the country. I couldn't see any phone shop letting me have a contract.'

Why didn't you just keep the phone contract you had at home? I wondered, then remembered a little sadly that we'd shared an EE account for over ten years, and he'd insisted on ending it when we separated. He wanted to be free of long-term ties to me.

You could always use my new address, I almost said, but stopped myself just in time, not only because I didn't want to sound needy. More importantly, I didn't want any long-term association of my address with his future life.

'I suppose I could have just got a pay-as-you-go, but I've no real need for a mobile phone,' he was saying. 'You know you can always contact me by email, and I'll pick any messages up next time I'm in an internet café.'

'Are internet cafés even still a thing, now that everyone has smartphones?'

He sighed. 'Oh Alice, you're so First World.' The line began to beep. 'Sorry, I'm out of change. But thanks again and do keep me posted about the other chess sets.'

'It would be a lot easier if you had a phone,' I began, but the line went dead. I'd just have to send an email to him and hope that wherever he was, he'd keep checking his inbox.

'Bye, Steven,' I said to thin air, wanting our parting to seem less abrupt.

As I trudged through the grass back to the kitchen, trying to disregard the dew creeping up the hem of my nightie, Mum waved to me through the window and pointed to her wristwatch.

Brace yourself, Nell, I thought wryly. *Here comes Mum.*

22

NELL'S MOVE

Although the flowers in my garden were no match for Robert's roses, I wanted to take some kind of floral offering to Nell. I hoped the sentimental value of knowing they had come from her old garden might make up for them being less flamboyant than my neighbour's showy blooms.

After a hasty shower, I took my kitchen scissors into the back garden and snipped an assortment of wildflowers, herbs and foliage and arranged them in a vintage jam jar of water, decorated with a strip of creamy, machine-made lace.

I'd judged correctly. Nell's face lit up when I set the jar down on her bedside table, her smile animating the many laughter lines on the papery skin around her eyes.

'Do you know, my dear, you are the first person to bring me flowers since you and young Bobby came to visit,' she said.

'Young Bobby?' Mum turned to me, her expression quizzical, perhaps now thinking I'd taken up with a toyboy.

Nell's twinkling eyes met Mum's. 'When you get to my age,

everyone's young. Besides, I've known Bobby Sponge since I was a relatively young woman, and he was a baby.'

'I thought SpongeBob was a recent creation,' replied Mum, even more perplexed.

Nell and I exchanged the companionable smile of those who share secrets.

'Just our silly village ways,' advised Nell. 'That's what we all call Bobby Praed in Little Pride because of his business. He's the Eternal Sponge fellow.'

'You know, Mum,' I added. 'The inventor of the everlasting washing-up sponge. His real name is Robert Praed. He's my next-door neighbour. Or rather, the house next door – his former childhood home – is one of his many properties. He kindly brought me to visit Nell when I first moved into Little Pride, so that I could ask her advice about the shop.'

Mum was speechless, but I could see her brain had gone into overdrive. I could almost hear wedding bells ringing in her ears.

Oh well, I thought, *at least if she knows a highly successful industrialist has got his country bolthole next to my shop, she might stop hinting for me to live with her.*

I took advantage of her silence to probe Nell very gently. 'Actually, Nell, there was something I wanted to ask you about the shop while I'm here. Did you ever have a rather strange customer, a chap on a motorbike, calling into the shop unannounced to buy and sell things at odd times outside of your opening hours?'

Nell tapped her fingers against her chin as she considered. 'Not that I recall, dear. What was his name?'

'I'm afraid I don't know. I didn't think to ask for his card.'

If he'd been one of Jack's chess-playing biker chums, with his nickname inscribed on the back of his leather jacket in metal studs, I'd surely have noticed. It wasn't inconceivable that he'd been at the sale at the school, didn't want to pay the asking price for one of the better sets, and thought it would be easier simply to pinch it under cover of darkness instead. If I hadn't been sleeping on the sofa, he might have got away with it.

'Your description of him rings no bells with me, my dear. As I told you when we first met, I kept my opening hours to suit myself, and if anyone wanted to visit my shop at any other time, they simply had to take it as a lesson in patience.'

I sighed. 'Perhaps I misunderstood what he said about you. Never mind, if he returns, I'll be sure to ask his name so I can remember him to you. He was a strange fellow.'

That was an understatement. I might be a rubbish liar, but I realised with a start that I was developing a talent for half-truths.

23

PROVENANCE

Cheered by our visit to Nell, and by learning about my wealthy widowed neighbour, Mum was less upset than she might have been when the police arrived on Monday evening to take statements from Danny and me. In an attempt to stop her eavesdropping, I sat her in the kitchen with Maudie's button box so the police could interview Danny and me out of her earshot in the sitting room. Even with her hearing aids, she would not have been able to listen to what we were saying through the closed door. I knew the button box would be as distracting as a set of Lego to a small child. Not for the first time, I was conscious of parenting the parent.

'Look, dear, this one's really old,' she piped up when I rejoined her in the kitchen during Danny's grilling. 'It must date back to way before plastic or even Bakelite. I wonder what it's made of? Whalebone, maybe, or ivory?'

I felt my face flush as I took it from her outstretched palm and held it up to the light.

'It's probably just bone, Mum.'

'Bone. Ivory. I suppose it's all the same, really, isn't it? All made of calcium, just occurring in different parts of the body.'

I tried to make light of her observation, so as not to betray the anxiety I was feeling at having only a door between this discussion of illegal substances and a pair of police officers.

'Just think, you could have saved my milk teeth to use as buttons for all those school cardigans you used to knit for me.'

'Perhaps that's what the tooth fairy does with them, dear.' She trilled with laughter, and I couldn't help but join in. 'Sells them on to knitters.'

I giggled. 'No wonder she pays so handsomely for them.'

When Mum reached her hand up to stroke my cheek fondly, I felt a frisson of familiar closeness. It was a gesture she had made every morning before I left for school and when tucking me into bed at night.

Even though I'd seen so little of her for so long, she was still my mum, and deep inside, I was still her little girl. With so much uncertainly around me right now, that meant more than I'd realised.

She reached for my hand and gave it an encouraging tug.

'Now, when you've finished with those coppers, tell me all about the rich chap who lives next door.'

* * *

'So, what do you make of the police's line of questioning?' I asked Danny once he'd shown the officers out.

'It seems they've already ruled out the group of bikers. In any case, it turns out they'd all been long gone by the time the murder happened, because they established that when the bikers drove off, the dead body wasn't in the car park. The bike was there, but no sign of its owner.'

'The police told you all that?' I was astonished. 'I thought they were meant to be questioning you, not the other way around.'

Danny smirked. 'They'd have to get up pretty early in the morning to outsmart me.' He puffed his chest out in mock pride, before exhaling to deflate it and laughing. 'No, to be honest, Alice, that was a bit of my own detective work. While you and Wendy were knitting by the fire yesterday evening, I took a stroll up to The Quarrymen's Arms to see whether I could pick up on how the local jungle drums are responding to Saturday's developments. I'm pleased to say I discovered something of crucial importance that the police hadn't yet spotted.'

He paused for effect.

'Go on,' I breathed. Danny's always been a good story-teller, much appreciated by the school parties who visit the museum.

'After leaving the sale, Malcolm Ashby' – the victim's real name, as we'd discovered from the visiting police – 'went to the pub.'

I thought for a moment while Danny, eyes twinkling, watched me, waiting for me to catch up with his train of thought.

'So, you're telling me he was on his own and not with the other bikers?'

Danny nodded. 'What's more, they've got evidence to prove that they left the village while he was still alive and in the pub.'

'You mean they were each other's alibis? Well, they would stand up for each other, wouldn't they?'

'Better than that. They've got the kind of trackers on their bikes that lorry drivers use to keep an accurate record of where they are and at what time, although they probably use them as a kind of travel diary, rather than for road safety issues. It's indisputable evidence, as they are tamperproof. So, they're all in the clear. Malcolm Ashby lingered in the pub till gone five. He was waiting to see the result of some horse race, apparently, according to Arthur.' Arthur was the landlord of The Quarrymen's Arms. 'The pub's television was showing the racing, and when a particular race came up, he took a betting slip out of his pocket, kissed it as if for good luck, then when his horse lost, ripped it in half and threw the pieces on the floor in anger.'

I screwed up my face in disappointment.

'So, the evidence will have been disposed of by now,' I concluded. 'They're bound to have swept the floor since Saturday afternoon.'

'Not necessarily. They might wait until the weekend rush is over and clean on Monday morning, when it would be so much quieter.'

I brightened. 'So if the ticket's still there, it might have his fingerprints on it to prove it was our biker.'

Danny raised his eyebrows at me. 'That would be handy. But if not, we've evidence enough without that, because some jolly old couple from the village got chatting to him. They should be able to identify him from a photo, as should Arthur, who served him.'

'Fabulous. Which couple?' I hoped they were reliable.

'Begins with a J,' said Danny, tapping his forehead as if that might help him remember.

'Jorkins?'

As if we were playing charades, he put a forefinger on his

nose and pointed to me with his other hand. 'That's it. Why, do you know them?'

'Yes, they were some of the first villagers to visit my shop on its opening day. They brought me home-grown, dried flowers to sell. Which reminds me, I've sold them all. I must settle up with them and see if they have any more I might sell, if it's not too late in the season.'

'Then you have the perfect excuse to visit the Jorkinses and fish for more information.'

I frowned, uncertain. 'Shouldn't we leave that to the police? You did tell them what you learned in the pub, didn't you?'

'Yes, of course. But from what you tell me about village life, I wonder whether an old couple like the Jorkinses might be more forthcoming to a local than to police detectives.'

'You may be right. Especially if I go to see them with the good news that I've come to give their share of the profits from their dried flower sales. But how will corroborating their evidence help us get any closer to finding Martin Ashby's murderer?'

'We don't know until we ask.'

'Then I'd better set about asking.' I looked at my watch: just coming up to 7 p.m. 'If the Jorkinses are as traditional as I think they are, Mrs Jorkins will have finished their tea and be in bed by nine. When I get back, I'll rustle up some tea for us to have with Mum. I won't be long with Mr and Mrs Jorkins. I've hardly had a chance to catch up with Mum properly since she's arrived.'

'Then perhaps it would be better if I make myself scarce for an hour or two, to give a chance for a bit of mother and daughter time. I don't want to play gooseberry.'

I wouldn't have thought of asking him to leave, but I was

very glad he'd offered, in his typically considerate way. Danny had been far too good for the selfish Martin. I hoped he'd not take long to find someone of equal kindness.

'But what will you do for your tea?' I asked, feeling slightly mean for so readily accepting his offer to depart.

He grinned. 'You're not the only one with a mother, you know. I'll take a leaf from your book and call in to spend a bit of quality time with my mum. She always rustles up something delicious whenever I turn up, unexpected or otherwise. Don't you worry about me, Alice. Now go and tell your plan to your mum.'

As good as gold, Mum was still in the little kitchen, sorting through Maudie's button box. Or rather selecting the ones that she fancied using for knitting projects. Since Mum had been on her own, after Dad died, she had knitted or crocheted all her Christmas presents, and I guessed she'd welcome the individual touch some of these buttons might provide for her gifts.

When I entered the kitchen, she looked up at me, slightly flushed with excitement.

I wondered how dull her life had become that she could get so worked up about a box of old buttons. Then I remembered how pleased I'd been to be able to buy them from Maudie. Besides, I was glad she was enjoying herself.

When I told her I was nipping out to see the Jorkinses, she set the buttons aside and leaped into action, insisting she'd have a nice meal ready for us on my return. Still weary from the turmoil of the last few days, I wasn't about to object.

24

THE JORKINS MANOEUVRE

The Jorkinses' cottage stood in Jubilee Lane, a row of tiny, terraced labourers' cottages built in the year of Queen Victoria's Diamond Jubilee.

To my relief, Mr and Mrs Jorkins were not at all put out by my impromptu visit. They invited me into their compact front parlour, where they'd been sitting in two floral fireside chairs bearing yellowing lace antimacassars. Mrs Jorkins insisted that I take her chair while she went to make us a pot of tea so strong that I could have used it to weatherproof my tea terrace tables.

Once she'd poured us each a cup, and added two spoons of sugar without asking if I wanted it, she perched on a rush-topped bentwood chair drawn from beneath their small dining table.

'All well with your shop, dearie?' began Mrs Jorkins. 'We noticed it wasn't open as usual when we went up to church for Matins on Sunday.'

Before I could reply, I had to unpucker my lips from the

cloying effect of my too-sweet tea. I haven't taken sugar since I was a teenager.

'Yes, fine, thank you. I just thought it better to keep it closed out of respect for the poor man who so sadly died in the school car park on Saturday.'

The old couple murmured sympathy.

'Such a shame, poor soul,' said Mrs Jorkins. 'Seemed such a nice young man. I hope it wasn't his bad luck on the horses that made him take his own life.'

'Gambling never did no one no good,' her husband interjected. 'Do you remember, Mrs Jorkins, that old fellow who hanged himself in the churchyard after losing all his savings at cards? It was the summer we bought this 'ere carpet.' He tapped a large orange sunflower, 1970s style, with the toe of his shoe. If the carpet was still this bright now, before many years of dust and dirt had been trodden in, it must have been dazzling in its heyday.

'This one didn't use a noose, though, did he?' put in Mrs Jorkins brightly. 'They say he ran himself over with that motorbike of his.'

I blinked, trying to picture how that might work. In my short time in Little Pride, I'd already learned how creative the village grapevine could be.

'I don't think so,' I said slowly. 'You see, I was one of the first people to see his dead body, and the cause of death was definitely a blow to the poor man's head.'

I gulped. It seemed rather unreal for me to have to say that.

'But of course that's all in the hands of the police now. They'll be organising a post-mortem as soon as they can, which will tell us what really happened. We can only speculate in the meantime.'

I paused, hoping my silence might prompt them to share any further details of their encounter with Malcolm Ashby. It worked.

Mrs Jorkins mopped some spilled tea from her saucer with a crumpled tissue pulled from the pocket of her yellow-and-red-checked apron. 'Well, whether this Mr Ashby killed hisself or someone else helped him on his way, I reckons it was down to money. Losing on that horse must have been the last straw that broke his back. Ruby Murray, it was called. He should have known better than to bet on a silly name like that. I reckons he didn't have two halfpennies to rub together, not once he'd bought his drop of brandy, anyway. See, I reckons he'd been pinching stuff from your chess show rather than pay for it. Maybe he was hoping to sell it to pay off gambling debts.'

'But how did you know when you weren't at the Chessmates launch yourselves?'

I doubted they'd have heard it from Tilly.

Mr Jorkins tapped his nose with his forefinger. 'Not much gets past Mrs Jorkins,' he said proudly. 'As I've learned to my cost in nearly sixty years of marriage.'

He winked amiably at his wife, who gave a girlish giggle.

'Not that he'd try to,' she said, before getting up to fetch from the dresser her handbag in the style of a saddlebag. 'I'm glad you called in tonight, my dear, as you've saved me a trip to bring this back to you.'

She unbuckled the bag and began to pull out various items while searching for the mystery object. Into the capacious lap of her apron, she decanted a couple of used tissues, an enamelled powder compact, a tiny bottle of eau-de-cologne and a fraying tweed purse, before producing with a flourish the unmistakeably chunky figure of an Isle of Lewis chess piece – one of the white knights. I wondered for a moment what the Vikings had called the knights. They weren't exactly known for their chivalry.

'Why else would a stranger be carrying around a chess piece in his pocket?' she cried in triumph. She held it out to me and dropped it into my palm. 'I'm right, aren't I? It is a chess piece? Though not like my old dad's wooden set back at home. It's quite a bit fancier. Might be worth a few bob, I suppose.'

I turned it over as if to inspect it, although there was no doubt in my mind that this was a white knight from Steven's Isle of Lewis set, riding astride its own chunky little horse.

'If Malcolm Ashby's aim was to sell it, he would have been disappointed,' I said, looking up. 'It's only a cheap imitation of a famous set in the British Museum. On its own, it would have been practically worthless. Not like some of the sets I was selling up at the school.'

'So I heard,' said Mr Jorkins. 'I hear the vicar paid over a hundred pounds for some fancy set. I don't know where the vicar gets that kind of money from, especially when he's always going on about fundraising for the bell tower.'

His wife pursed her lips. 'Now, Mr Jorkins, don't you go casting aspersions on the vicar. He is allowed money of his own to spend, you know. He gets paid a wage like everyone else in employment; he doesn't do it only for love. Besides, you can't expect him to put all his own money into preserving the church. It's not like he owns it. Now, hush with you, or Alice will be thinking the vicar's had his hand in the collection plate, and you know no such thing.' She turned to me with her brow furrowed in concern. 'That's how rumours start.'

I raised my hands in surrender. 'Don't worry, I don't

believe that for a moment. But tell me, how did you come to have the chess piece in your handbag if it was originally in the dead man's possession?'

'It fell out of his trouser pocket when he pulled out his betting slip, and it rolled across the floor to beneath the table where Mr Jorkins and I were sitting enjoying our Saturday lunchtime stouts.' Seeing my puzzled look, she elaborated. 'A pint of stout for him and a half for me, every Saturday afternoon, keeps us topped up with iron and all sorts. Drank it when I was expecting too, like the midwife told me to, and our boy Derek is six foot three now, which just goes to show...'

Mr Jorkins, all of five foot six, sat up taller in his chair, as if making a subtle claim that his genes, and not just the stout, had played a part in determining Derek's height.

'But when I got up from our table while Mr Jorkins was returning our empties to the bar, and went to give the fellow his chess piece, he took one look at it and ran for the door. I suppose it was being confronted with the evidence of his theft that shamed him.'

'Either that or he thought you was about to make a citizens' arrest,' chortled her husband. Her short, squat figure can't have posed much of a threat to a man of Malcolm Ashby's stature in biking leathers, but I still wouldn't have liked to get on the wrong side of this determined old soul.

'Anyhow, when he made off like that, I decided I wasn't going to bother running after him.'

I wondered when Mrs Jorkins had last run anywhere.

'The way he took on made me sure he must have half-inched it at your show,' she continued. 'So, I dropped it into my handbag – I never goes anywhere without this 'ere handbag – until such time as I could return it to its rightful owner.'

'Which would be you,' Mr Jorkins added helpfully, lest I was in any doubt.

She laid it gently on my outstretched palm.

'Thank you very much,' I replied. 'Of course I'd be unable to sell any sets with missing pieces, so I really appreciate your thoughtfulness.'

Mr Jorkins wagged a finger at me. 'They does that with jigsaw puzzles all the time in village jumble sales, mind. You look like the puzzling type.' I decided to take that as a compliment. 'So, there's a word of warning for you. Never buy a jigsaw from a jumble sale unless you have time to count all the pieces first.'

'Still, at least with a chess set, it's a lot easier to count the pieces than with a jigsaw,' I said, as I got to my feet and set my empty teacup and saucer on the fender. 'Thank you very much for the tea, but I'd better be getting home now. My mother arrived last night to stay for a few days, and I'd better get back to her.'

'Why, you would have been welcome to bring her too,' cried Mrs Jorkins. 'Perhaps another time, my dear.'

I looked around the tiny, crowded room, wondering where on earth Mum could have sat. Mrs Jorkins beamed, reading my mind.

'Although she might have had to sit on Mr Jorkins's lap.'

As she giggled, her husband patted the shiny thighs of his baggy trousers.

'Ah, but I've only ever had knees for my wife.' He winked at her again.

'Ooh hoo!' she shrieked in girlish delight.

Perhaps I was leaving at just the right time.

25

KNIGHT ERRANT

'Why would anyone steal a single chess piece?' mused Mum as I explained the outcome of my visit to the Jorkins while we knitted by the fire together. 'It's of even less use than stealing a single earring. Or maybe that's a bad example. There was that famous girl with the pearl earring, wasn't there? Didn't she just have the one? Didn't do her any harm, I suppose.'

'You mean the Vermeer painting, Mum?' I said with a smile. 'I suppose it is a bit odd that its title only mentions the one earring you can see. I'll never look at that painting in the same way again. I'll always be wondering whether she's got a matching pearl earring in her other ear now.'

'I've always thought she looked a bit shifty,' said Mum. 'Perhaps she'd pinched it.'

'And the painting was the Renaissance equivalent of a police mugshot showing her in possession of the evidence?' I laughed.

We were still giggling when Danny let himself into the shop and through to join us in the sitting room.

'Before you ask, I have locked the shop door behind me,'

he said, slipping his jacket off and hanging it on a hook by the back door.

His remark sobered me a little. Although waking up to find an intruder had been unpleasant, it was only after it was all over that it occurred to me how much worse it might have been if Mum had insisted on sleeping on the sofa instead of accepting my room. Supposing he'd assaulted her – or worse?

As Danny slumped down onto the sofa beside me, he noticed for the first time the Isle of Lewis knight in splendid isolation in the middle of the coffee table, where I'd set it down on my return from the Jorkinses'. While chatting to Mum, I'd been fiddling with the button box, and the white knight now stood proudly in the centre of concentric circles of antique and vintage buttons, arranged in rainbow order. Danny pointed at him.

'You look like you're making a tiny pagan god for the Borrowers to worship,' he remarked. 'But hang on, isn't that one of the pieces that Tilly said Malcolm Ashby stole? Where did that come from?'

I straightened my back, proud of my achievement. 'Yes, I've just redeemed it from the Jorkinses. Apparently, our murder victim dropped it in the pub and when Mrs Jorkins tried to return it to him, he fled. She guessed where it had come from and kept it to return to me.'

Danny considered for a moment. 'I suppose anyone who knew about the Chessmates event, which was all the village, might have done the same.'

Mum leaned forward. 'Or maybe there was someone else in the pub who he didn't want to know he had it for another reason.'

Danny and I sat bolt upright, startled by Mum's deduction. Maybe I'd inherited my sleuthing instincts from her.

'You mean there was more than one person after those particular chess pieces that afternoon?' said Danny. 'And he wanted to keep it hidden from a theoretical rival?'

I reached across the coffee table, intending to pick the knight up, then retracted my outstretched arm in a hurry.

'What on earth was I thinking? I should have been handling this piece with gloves or a tissue, so as not to destroy any forensic evidence it might hold.' I paused for thought. 'Although as it's already been in Malcolm Ashby's trouser pocket, rolled across the sticky floor of The Quarrymen's Arms, and nestled in the bottom of Mrs Jorkins's jumbled handbag, it will be so contaminated that I don't suppose there's much point.'

I picked it up again and cradled it in my hand on its back. It reminded me of the characters in *Noggin the Nog*, the vintage children's television animation by Oliver Postgate and Peter Firmin.

'Actually, I reckon there's more to this set than meets the eye, and it's nothing that fingerprints would tell us,' I said slowly. 'Bearing in mind Tilly reckons her opponent pinched loads of the pieces, he had the others on his person somewhere, and he may have packed the rest of them in his motorbike panniers after he left the school hall. After all, he couldn't drive off with them in his pockets. If they tumbled out while he was speeding along a country lane, he'd never find them again. And that's why whoever killed him rooted through his pockets and his panniers and took what they could find, not realising Mrs Jorkins had already taken one home in her handbag.'

I picked the knight up between finger and thumb as if about to interrogate it.

'Ha!' said Mum. 'You remind me of the drawing in

Through the Looking Glass where Alice has just rescued the White King from among the cinders in the hearth.'

'Yes, just after she's rescued the White Queen and their pawn, baby Lily,' I recalled. '"The White Knight is sliding down the poker. He balances very badly".' I quoted the words that Alice wrote in her memorandum book. I addressed the knight in my hand. 'I'm guessing that the set you came from is every bit as special as Alice's in Looking-Glass World. Our challenge now is to find out what made it so special – and valuable enough for someone to kill the original thief so that they could steal the pieces from him.'

'So, what next?' asked Mum, as absorbed in this quest now as Danny and me.

'We should check its provenance statement,' advised Danny. 'The very least it can tell us is who Steven originally bought it from. Perhaps the previous owner might be able to shed some light on the mystery.'

I fell back against the sofa, feeling slightly daunted by the task ahead.

'Wouldn't it be foolhardy to reveal to a stranger that we still have the rest of the set in our possession? If someone has already killed to acquire part of it, might they do so again to nab the remaining pieces?'

'Good point, Alice.' Danny rubbed his chin in thought. 'Although we don't have to tell them that, do we? We can just tell them the whole set has been stolen. Then no one would bother coming here to look for the rest of it.'

'Whatever you decide to tell them, you can do that tomorrow,' said Mum, getting to her feet. 'What you need, young lady, is another early night to regain your strength.'

26

IN SEARCH OF THE KING

While Mum made us all some bedtime cocoa, Danny and I found the paperwork that Steven had kept with the Isle of Lewis chess set. I was relieved to see my memory was correct. This was one of the cheap sets that he'd bought because he liked the look of it, rather than because of its rarity or novelty value. This kind of purchase was likely to decrease in value rather than appreciate every time it changed hands. Most of Steven's purchases for his collections were made on emotional or sentimental grounds rather than as shrewd business investments. But I didn't mind that. He only ever spent what he could afford on his various whims, and his acquisitiveness was just a hobby. It was cluttering up the house with his collections that I found hard to live with. Even so, I took his untidy habits as licence to treat myself to craft materials whenever I wanted – my equivalent compulsion. Looking back, I wondered if he'd secretly been as dismissive of my purchases as I was of his. It was odd how, now that he was out of my life, I was getting to know him better than ever before.

To be fair, there were more expensive and annoying hobbies that his friends pursued – following a football team, playing golf, even gliding. But at least those pursuits never cluttered up their homes. His best friend, Christo, was never going to park his glider in the lounge of his family home.

'An eBay purchase,' I said as I scanned the details of the top sheet of a stapled sheaf of papers. 'I thought so. He only paid thirty quid for it. Why would anyone think such a cheap set worth stealing?'

'Or murdering for,' added Danny in a low voice. 'Especially when there were far more valuable sets on display at the side of the hall. All of those are intact. It doesn't add up.'

'I supposed Malcolm Ashby might just have been ignorant or ill-informed. But there were price labels, Danny. It's not as if we'd kept the values hidden. Surely he didn't think it was the original set from the British Museum? No one could be that daft.'

We were silent for a moment.

'Of course, the chess set might be a complete red herring,' I said slowly. 'Or rather, a black-and-white one.'

Danny grimaced at my bad joke. 'You mean there could have been a different motive for his murder? I suppose so. I suspect the police will be investigating all lines of enquiry, checking him out on the national crime database, and so on. But it can't hurt to find out more about the chess set, just in case it is the reason for the assault. I can't quite think what that might be, but I must admit I'm intrigued.'

'Me too,' I agreed. 'So, let's try and contact the person he bought it from to see whether they can shed any light on the mystery. Maybe they're still trading on eBay.'

I fetched my laptop from the kitchen and fired it up. Navigating to eBay, I searched for the vendor's identity, as listed on the receipt.

'Kingcharles35701521,' I read aloud. 'Wow, maybe it's the fact that it belonged to the King that makes it so desirable.'

Danny laughed. 'There are people out there gullible enough to believe that. Maybe someone is hoping to clone the King using DNA taken off his supposed chess pieces.'

'Goodness, they might have ended up cloning an extra Steven instead.' I clapped my hand to my mouth in mock horror. 'One Steven in my life is more than enough.'

'I bet the police haven't thought of pursuing that line of enquiry,' said Danny. 'Anyway, I hate to disappoint you, but we didn't have a king at the time Steven bought this. The King was still Prince Charles then, so that puts paid to that theory.'

'You're right. So, let's track down this kingcharles35701521. Whoever he is, it can't hurt to contact him.'

A search on eBay for his identity drew a blank. Presumably, he'd deleted his account since selling the chess set to Steven.

But when I slapped the receipt face down on the coffee table in frustration, my disappointment turned to hope.

'Look, Danny, that's Steven's handwriting on the back. He's jotted down a telephone number. What are the chances it's related to this purchase?'

'There's one way to find out. Odd that it's a landline, though. Habitual sellers would be more likely to give mobile numbers rather than landlines so that buyers can text them.'

'Maybe kingcharles35701521 is over a certain age and hasn't got into smartphones,' I suggested. 'Or he lives in a mobile signal blackspot. There are still a few of them left.'

'Would you like me to make the call for you?' Danny

offered. 'I could pretend to be Steven with a question about the chess set.'

I shook my head. 'Thanks, that's kind of you, but a female voice might offer a softer approach and be less likely to be rebuffed without really engaging.'

'Can you do a Geordie accent?' he asked. 'I think that's meant to be the most liked voice on customer service helplines.'

I laughed. 'Yes, I'm not sure I could sustain it under stress. But more importantly, what should I say? I don't want to come straight out with and tell them their old chess set might have got someone killed. That might just make them clam up. But you know I'm a terrible liar.'

Danny thought for a moment. 'You can speak truthfully without telling them everything. Just say you're investigating an attempted theft of the set and wondering why anyone would bother with it when it's of no value, and whether it had previously belonged to someone famous that might make it collectible.'

I flicked through the few sheets stapled to the eBay receipt.

'There's nothing there to suggest that.' Then I had a brainwave. 'I could tell them I don't have the paperwork to hand, and I'm wondering whether they still have details of the set that they could forward to me.'

Danny ripped the stapled attachments off the back of the eBay receipt and sat on them before passing just the receipt back to me.

'There you go. Now you'll be speaking the truth. So, dial the number quick, before you lose your nerve.'

I glanced at the clock. It was gone ten.

'I'll try first thing tomorrow, before I open the shop,' I decided, glad to have a little more time to build up my courage.

27

ENCOUNTERING QUEENIE

Next morning, at 9.30 a.m., I ventured out into the garden again with my phone. Once I'd finished dialling, I half expected to get the unobtainable tone or a voicemail message. Even if someone did answer it, I might be no further forward. After all, it was a few years since the transaction had taken place. Besides, if the seller was a commercial trader, he might have no recollection of Steven's purchase. It could be one of thousands.

When I heard the ringing tone at the other end, I held my breath until someone picked up.

'Queenie,' said a woman's voice, sounding rather flat. 'Is that you, Eileen? You've come up as "unknown caller", and you said you were getting a new phone.'

I guessed Queenie didn't get many phone calls. Maybe her thick lisp made her self-conscious over the phone.

'Hello, Queenie,' I began, glad to know her first name already, which would help me sound more friendly and warm. 'No, it's not Eileen. This is Alice. We've not met before.'

'I don't take cold calls from people trying to sell me stuff,' she said briskly. 'Where'd you get my number anyway? It ain't right calling people's home phones to sell them stuff outside office hours.'

I replied as quickly as I could, fearing she might hang up on me before I could get to the point.

'No, no, don't worry, I'm not trying to sell you anything. I'm just following up a purchase my partner made from' – I glanced at the receipt – 'someone going by the eBay identity of kingcharles35701521 with this landline as his phone contact.'

There was a silence long enough for me to wonder whether the line had gone dead. Then the woman piped up again.

'OK, fair do's. So you want Chas?' I remembered Chas was the old-fashioned abbreviation for Charles. 'Then you're out of luck. I'm Queenie King, his other half. Well, they all started called me Queenie after Prince Charles got made King. The King's wife, you know. Fair do's.'

I gave a polite titter. 'I see. Very good.' I tried to put her at her ease with a joke of my own. 'I suppose they could just have easily called you Camilla.'

To my relief, she found that notion hilarious.

'I hadn't thought of that,' she continued, after recovering from a fit of laughter. 'Fair do's. I wouldn't have minded that. I like old Camilla. Anyway, if you're wanting to talk to Chas, you're out of luck. He's long gone.'

Presuming Chas had abandoned her as Steven had me, I felt a twinge of fellow feeling for Queenie. I pictured Chas and Steven merrily zooming off to India – or wherever Steven was by now – on their motorbikes together, or perhaps Chas travelling in a sidecar, with the lightest of luggage and not a care in the world, leaving Queenie and me to deal with the fallout of their departures.

'Dead and buried,' continued Queenie, matter-of-fact. 'Not that he's any great loss to me. Four years come Friday he's been gone.'

I checked the date of the eBay transaction. Steven had bought the chess set just a few days before Chas's demise.

'I'm sorry,' I said, as much for her loveless marriage as for her husband's death.

'So, I don't suppose I'm much help to you, then?' she replied, her voice softening.

I thought it was worth gently pressing her further.

'If you're sure you don't mind me asking,' I began, my heart beating a little faster. 'It's about a chess set Chas sold to my ex-partner Steven not quite four years ago.'

I heard Queenie gasp, but she kept her voice steady. 'He sold a lot of chess sets, lovey. And backgammon, and that funny Chinese game like dominoes, only different, all sorts of fancy games he couldn't play. Give me bingo any day, I used to say to him. At least then you stand a chance of winning a prize, but he took no notice. He said he just liked the glamour of the import-export trade. Not that it seemed very glamorous to me.'

'I'm not sure this set would have been a foreign import,' I said slowly, thinking on my feet. 'It was a modern reproduction of one in the British Museum – the Isle of Lewis chess set.'

There was an uncomfortable silence, and I feared we'd been cut off.

'Alice.' It was the first time she'd used my name, and there was an urgent sincerity in her voice. 'Alice, I remember that one, and it won't be worth nothing now. When's your next bin day?'

That was an odd question, but I answered it anyway. 'Friday.'

'Well, Alice, if I was you, this Friday, I'd chuck it in your dustbin rather than keep it in your house. I know the set you mean, and I reckon there's a curse on it. My old man went bananas when I sent it off to your fella. I used to do all the packing and sending for the stuff what he sold, and I handled the phone calls and emails too. He said I'd sent it to the wrong Steven. It weren't my fault, it was just bad luck that there were two fellas with the same name in the list of buyers that day, and I'd sent them each other's sets by mistake. Both identical sets, though I don't see it mattered. When I said to Chas, "Thirty quid of anyone's money is still thirty quid," he fetched me such a whack around the ear, I passed out cold. He was that sort of a bloke, a bit hasty when cross, but next day he always said sorry and bought me flowers or scent or the like. Our boy's just the same. But this time, he didn't get a chance to apologise.' In her stride now, she paused for effect. 'Because the day after, Chas was found stone dead in the street, knocked down by a hit-and-run driver. The police never got to the bottom of it, but I reckon they didn't try. My Chas hadn't always been on the right side of the law, see, so they probably thought good riddance to bad rubbish, and I can't say I disagreed.'

'Goodness,' was my inadequate response. Whatever I'd been expecting, it wasn't another brutal murder.

'So, call me superstitious, but I blamed that chess set, see. I never liked the look of those funny little men. They looked like demons to me. So I decided to get rid of all trace of it and chucked the paperwork on the fire. That felt so good that I burned the rest of his old files too, and I deleted his eBay and email accounts. Fair do's.'

That made sense to me.

'I didn't want to keep up his trade anyway. It didn't give me no pleasure. Gave what was left of his stock back to Eric Vyse, the bloke who shipped them in for him, and I wouldn't take nothing for it either, I was that glad to be shot of it. Went out and got myself a job behind the bar at the local, and that gives me all the money I need to get by, and good company too.'

'That was very generous of you.'

I felt genuine sympathy, and somewhat in awe of her determination. She'd clearly had a tough time with the dreadful Chas, but she'd successfully reinvented herself. Quite the inspiration. Plus, what she was telling me was pure gold. The police would never have made this connection without Danny, Mum and me uncovering it.

'You may say so, but Eric Vyse didn't think so. Even insisted on searching my flat to make sure I hadn't kept any stuff back, cheeky monkey. Still, he didn't find nothing. What's gone is gone, I told him. From the look on his face when he realised he'd have to lump it, anyone else would have thought he was about to bash me too. But I had something on him, see. I'd had a fling with him before I was with Chas, and I knew he'd never lay a finger on me in case I blabbed about it to his missus. Fair do's.' Her voice dropped to a whisper. 'Though all the same, I tipped the police off to check Eric Vyse's car bumpers to see whether it was him what done my Chas in. I don't suppose they did, though. Last I heard of Eric Vyse, he was lording in up on the Costa del Sol. Them Spaniards are welcome to him, as far as I'm concerned.' She paused for a much-needed breath. 'So that's that. Anything else I can help you with, lovey?'

Unburdening herself to me seemed to have softened her further.

'No, no thank you,' I said. 'But you've been very kind and helpful. More than I could have expected, and I'm very grateful. I'd love to send you some flowers to say a proper thank you, if you wouldn't mind giving me your postal address?'

As soon as the words were out of my mouth, the line went dead.

28

A PAWN IS TAKEN

It was a relief to return to a normal routine for the rest of the day. As I prepared to open the Curiosity Shop at 10 a.m., the events of Saturday seemed like a figment of my imagination. While rearranging the shop windows, cleared now of chess sets, I watched the schoolchildren head up the high street towards the school. Memories of Mum walking me to my primary school came flooding back, causing a pang of regret that I'd never have a child of my own to share that experience.

Before I could become too maudlin, Mum distracted me with a flurry of questions about the shop. Pleased that she was taking such an interest, I realised I'd been silly to expect her to disapprove of my new venture. I took pride in showing her the before-and-after photos of the shop. I'd taken quite a few of how shabby and grubby it was when I'd moved in, thinking at the time that they'd be useful for planning how I'd transform the shop into living space. Now the pictures reassured me of the progress I'd made updating the shop while keeping true to traditional rural values. Cynics might dismiss it as trendy cottagecore, but to me it had authenticity and heart, not least because much of the stock was locally sourced.

The flow of customers was much busier than on a usual Tuesday morning, most of them locals wanting to hear my version of Saturday's events. Careful to avoid fuelling local rumour that might hamper the police investigation, I didn't reveal anything that had happened after the police had arrived in the school car park. I probably wasn't telling them anything they didn't already know, but they seemed satisfied at getting the details first-hand. Most made at least a minor purchase out of politeness to show their appreciation.

Late morning, Mum insisted on minding the shop while I popped up to Suki's Stores for a few groceries. She enjoyed playing with the vintage till, opening and closing it far more times than was necessary for the couple of sales she had made so far.

Suki, of course, was all ears about Malcolm's murder, but had nothing useful to add.

'At least when people stay at home playing games on their computers, they don't get murdered in school car parks,' she said.

I didn't think that was entirely fair, but I knew better than to argue with Suki.

When I got back to the shop, I insisted on making lunch for Mum after she'd done all the cooking the previous day, but it was a relatively late lunch by the time I carried our plates of ham salad rolls out onto the tea terrace. Fortunately, the flagstones had been soaking up the pale, autumn sunshine all day, so it was warmer than it looked out there, and sitting outside in the fresh air for a breather did us both good.

I returned from fetching us a second cup of coffee to find Robert sitting in my chair, deep in conversation with Mum, who was clearly charmed by him. I could relate to that. Seeing him smiling at something Mum had just said gave me a surprising twinge of jealousy. *He's mine*, was my first thought, which instantly I dismissed as ridiculous. Although Robert was about ten years old than me, Mum was at least fifteen years older than him, possibly even old enough to be his mother if she'd started young, as women did in her heyday. Feeling foolish, I set the coffees on the table. Robert, ever the gentleman, leaped to his feet.

'Sorry, Alice, I didn't mean to pinch your seat.'

I raised my hand and gestured to lower him again. 'No problem, I can easily bring over another chair. Would you like a coffee too? It's no trouble.'

He gave me a warm smile. 'Thank you, that would be very nice. You know how I like it.'

Mum's mouth made a silent O, and her cheeks pinkened as she flashed me a conspiratorial look. I turned abruptly away, rolling my eyes in despair. Of course she wasn't after Robert for herself; she was just surreptitiously interviewing him as a potential son-in-law. I sighed. She never changed, but I supposed that wasn't all bad.

When I returned with Robert's coffee, Mum was cradling in her hand a free sample of his original product: the Eternal Sponge that had set Robert on the path to success as an innovative industrialist, making his fortune – and improving the lives of washers-up all over the world – by reinventing humble domestic products.

And there was me thinking Robert had been chatting me up those few months ago when he pressed a similar sample into my hand. It was just his salesman's patter after all.

For a while, we made polite small talk about where Mum lived in Norfolk and how different it was over that side of the country, and the pros and cons of village life, until the sound of the end-of-day school bell drifted down the high street on the breeze to us. I glanced at my watch.

'Not that I want to get rid of you, Robert,' I began. Mum shot me a glance that said she didn't want me to either. 'But aren't you collecting Tilly from school today?'

Robert sat back and put his hands behind his head. 'Nope, it's a day off for Grandpa today. Belinda's picking her up to take her to a hairdresser's appointment in town. For some reason, she doesn't trust Coralie to cut her hair or me to instruct a hairdresser. I don't know why. Tilly's hair is far too beautiful for me to allow anything drastic to happen to it. It's still quite fine, almost like baby hair, although there's a lot more of it now than the peach fuzz she had when she was born.'

Mum smiled. 'You sound just like my late husband,' she said. 'Once he even pretended to take Alice to the hairdresser's when I asked him to, but he couldn't bring himself to do it because he couldn't bear to see her baby curls cut off. I'm not quite sure how he thought he'd get away with it. I mean, me, her mother, who brushed her hair every morning and evening. How would I not notice there wasn't any less of it?'

A throng of young voices was getting louder as the schoolchildren spilled out onto the high street and dispersed into the surrounding lanes. Several children waved and shouted in greeting as they whizzed past us on their scooters, followed by a couple of girls skipping enthusiastically, long ponytails leaping about as if they had a life of their own.

'How lucky you are to have a little granddaughter so close by,' Mum was saying.

I cringed. So far on this visit, she'd avoided any mention of her thwarted grandmotherly feelings, and I didn't want her to start now, especially in front of Robert.

Robert was as gracious and diplomatic as ever.

'Young Tilly's a bit of a handful sometimes,' he told her. 'But you can borrow her any time you like. The best thing about grandchildren is that you can give them back.'

He wasn't fooling either of us. But before we could respond, a white four-by-four screeched to a halt outside Robert's house next door.

'That's Belinda's car,' said Robert, getting to his feet. 'I expect Tilly's refusing to go to the hairdresser's again, and Belinda wants me to tell her she must.'

As he went down to the roadside to greet them, Belinda leaped out of the driver's seat, her car door nearly knocking over a couple of older children freewheeling on their bikes down the middle of the road.

'Had you forgotten I said I'd pick Tilly up today? I was taking a couple of hours off work especially. Now, where is she? We're going to be late for the hair salon.'

Robert laid a calming hand on Belinda's shoulders. 'No, darling, I remembered.'

'Then where is she?'

'I don't know, darling. Have you checked with a member of staff at the school? Perhaps she's waiting inside.'

'Yes, of course I have, and she's not.'

Mum, who had been frowning at Belinda's shortness with her father, now began to look agitated.

'Are you sure she hasn't just sneaked off to the playpark or gone home with a little friend to avoid having her hair cut?' asked Robert. 'We know she has form on that score.' A tremor had crept into his voice. 'Surely the teacher on playground duty will know. They don't let any of the children leave the school with any person not known to them.'

Belinda clutched her head with both hands. 'That's just it. The teacher on duty, Miss blinking Blinken, was distracted by some little wretch who had just projectile-vomited across the bicycle rack. They were so busy trying to tend to the pesky vomiter and console the kids whose bikes and scooters he'd just pebble-dashed that she'd lowered her guard. She told me Tilly had been picked up and driven off by her grandmother in her green, open-top sports car. Of course, everyone knows your pesky midlife crisis car by sight, but you never pick her up by car, and no one would mistake you for an old woman. You always walk up so you can spoil her in Suki's Stores on the way home. Or now in Alice's Cotswold Curiosity Shop too.' She turned to glare at me as if, somehow, I was to blame for Tilly's disappearance. 'Besides, Dad's car is still in his driveway.'

Mum got to her feet and led Belinda to an empty chair, pushing her down into the seat. 'Let me get you a cup of tea, dear, while you phone round her friends' mums. I'm sure she'll turn up at a friend's house.'

'Add a shot of gin to it, will you?' Belinda called after Mum as she headed indoors.

I knew Mum would ignore her request, given Belinda was driving.

I closed my eyes as the thought occurred to me that perhaps this stranger had hired the same make and model as Robert's in order to fool the teachers that she was his sister or similar, sent by Robert to collect Tilly in his place.

Before I could pursue that thought, Herbie Studge came careering down the pavement on his scooter, clutching something in his right hand. I hoped he'd learned his lesson from our first encounter not to use his mobile phone while scooting. But I'd misjudged him. He wasn't holding his phone, but a small, manila envelope.

'Mr Sponge,' he panted. 'A lady in a green car like yours just asked me to give you this letter. She paid me a fiver to deliver it to you. Is it OK for me to keep the fiver or do you think she meant for me to give you that as well? She drove off before I could ask her. Mrs Frampton shook her fist at the lady for driving so fast. She does that to me sometimes too when I'm on my scooter.'

Robert took the envelope from him and tore it open, waving the proffered five-pound note aside. He marched over to the far corner of the tea terrace for privacy in which to read it.

Apparently wrestling with his conscience, Herbie looked to me for guidance. I thought quickly. Perhaps the fiver would have the driver's fingerprints on it. It was surely the driver of the green sports car that had bribed Herbie to deliver the note.

'I think the lady meant the fiver to be your reward,' I told him. 'But I tell you what, Herbie, I'd like to reward you for being so helpful too. Come into the shop with me, and I'll swap your fiver for a tenner.'

Herbie's eyes grew as round as the wheels on his scooter. 'Wow, thanks, miss. I might start helping more people if it earns me such a fortune.'

Once inside the shop, I indicated to Herbie to lay his fiver on the counter, so I would not contaminate it with my own prints. When I opened the till and passed him a tenner, he asked what else he could do to help. I gave him a piece of paper and a pencil.

'Go outside and sit at one of the tea tables, and write

down everything you remember about the lady who gave you the letter for Mr Sponge, and about her car too.'

Herbie frowned, puzzled. 'The lady told me she was going to be getting married to Mr Sponge, so won't Mr Sponge know all about her already? She said she was going to be Tilly's new grandma. She'd given Tilly a bag of lollipops, and Tilly gave one of them to me.' He patted his pocket, making me briefly glad that he hadn't tried eating his lollipop while scooting – another accident waiting to happen. 'Tilly said she liked her.'

I closed my eyes briefly in horror at this further evidence of abduction. 'I'm sorry, Herbie, but that lady wasn't being truthful. Mr Sponge's wife sadly died a few years ago, and he doesn't have any plans to marry another lady, as far as I know. However, your description could help us find out who she really is.'

And help us get Tilly back, I said inwardly, while trying to keep alive a shred of hope that this was just a harmless misunderstanding.

Herbie chewed the end of the pencil in thought as I followed him out of the shop and onto the tea terrace, where he turned to me apologetically.

'I'm not very good at spelling,' he said.

'Doesn't matter,' I replied firmly. 'Neither was Sherlock Holmes. Why do you think Dr Watson wrote up all his cases?'

I'd made that up, but it had the desired effect. Newly appointed consulting detective Herbie Studge sat down and began to write rapidly.

Leaving him to it, I headed back to the terrace. Belinda was sitting where Mum had left her, slumped in her chair, biting her perfectly manicured nails. Seated beside her, Robert was staring bleakly into the distance, the letter dangling from his hand. As I approached, he turned to greet me, his face pale and drawn. It was as if he'd aged ten years in five minutes.

'It's a ransom note,' he murmured. 'They've taken Tilly and will only return her...' His voice cracked, and he took a moment to recover the power of speech. Knowing how rich Robert was, I expected the note to demand a huge sum of money. 'If you give them your Isle of Lewis chess set,' he finished. He gazed at me, bewildered. 'Why on earth would they want that?' he added. 'And why go to such cruel lengths to secure it? Don't they know who I am?'

I laid a comforting hand on his arm. 'I'd give all of my chess sets and the entire contents of my shop to get Tilly back for you. But I'm afraid that particular chess set is incomplete. Some pieces have already been stolen. I simply don't have them.'

29

MORE MISSING PIECES

To my astonishment, Robert broke out into a huge grin.

'Stolen? Actually, I'd like to think they've just been borrowed. You see, Alice, I know exactly where they are, and I shall return them to you right now. They're all tucked away in the Sylvanian double-decker bus that I keep at my house for Tilly to play with. I was going to make her bring them back to you tomorrow after I picked her up from school and apologise to you for being so naughty as to steal them at the Chessmates event on Saturday. But I didn't know they were in my house until my cleaning lady discovered them while dusting the playroom a little while ago. We had a good laugh about it. The chessmen looked so funny in among Tilly's Sylvanian badgers and foxes and the rest. Not that I'm condoning Tilly's behaviour for a moment.'

Belinda stared at him, open-mouthed.

'My daughter's no thief,' she faltered.

'How many?' I asked. In my eagerness to recover the missing pieces, I had no time to pander to Belinda's hurt pride. 'How many did she take?'

'Just the four that I spotted. The standard Sylvanian family unit: a mummy, a daddy and two children. I mean, the king and queen and a couple of pawns. I take it you have the rest?'

I shook my head slowly. 'I'm afraid I don't. I've recovered one missing white knight, thanks to Mr and Mrs Jorkins's vigilance, but I'm afraid ten of the white pieces stolen by Malcolm Ashby, the man murdered on Saturday, are still missing. My theory is that someone murdered him in order to steal the ones he'd taken.'

Robert's jaw dropped. 'But why? They're worthless bits of plastic, probably worth even less than the same number of Sylvanians. Or are they actually some rare antique made of some fabulously valuable material? I thought you were only allowing the children to play with the cheaper, modern sets.'

'They're pure, unadulterated plastic,' I confirmed. 'Danny and I tested all the sets before the sale.'

Robert shook his head in puzzlement. 'So why would anyone ask for them as a ransom when they must know I'm worth millions in ready money?'

'You're worth billions, Pa, if you include all your assets,' Belinda corrected him.

Mum, emerging from the shop with Belinda's cup of tea, let out a little squeal at Belinda's revelation.

'Then we'll just have to give them the pieces we still have and hope that will be enough,' I said, trying to sound more positive than I felt. 'Perhaps they already have the ones that Malcolm Ashby had pinched, because it seems someone stole them from him, and murdered him in the process.'

We were all silent for a moment at that awful thought.

'And if not, I could ask whether they'll accept some cash

as compensation for the missing pieces,' added Robert. 'But first, I think we had better alert the police.'

30

THE ROUND-UP

Leaving Mum in charge of the shop and of Herbie still
scribbling away, I searched out the remaining pieces of the
chess set while Robert led a sobbing Belinda, his arms
around her, into his house. By the time I'd found them and
was about to head next door, I could hear a siren hurtling
down the high street. I wondered whether Maudie Frampton
would shake her fist at the police car for speeding.

A police car pulled up behind Belinda's four-by-four just
as I reached the pavement. The two police officers, different
ones from the pair who'd been involved with the investigation
over the weekend, stepped out onto the pavement, seeming to
know their way into his house. I followed them in, closing the
high gates behind us. As an exceptionally wealthy resident,
Robert may have already been on their radar as being at risk
of various crimes, kidnap included.

Robert was standing at the open front door to meet them.

'Please come in, Officers, Alice.' Even at this time of crisis,
his perfect manners did not desert him.

He led us into the sitting room, where I laid the chess

pieces on the coffee table. Robert acknowledged them with a sad smile that didn't reach his eyes.

Belinda was sitting, blank-faced, on the sofa, staring at a crumpled tissue in her hands. I passed her a clean tissue from my pocket and laid a hand on her shoulder in moral support. Without looking at me, she nodded in silent thanks.

'Alice, could you please do me a favour?' he asked me. 'Go up to the playroom and fetch Tilly's Sylvanian bus.'

The police officers exchanged glances that suggested they thought he'd lost the plot, but I ignored them and did as Robert said.

'First on the left on the top landing,' he called after me.

He must have realised I'd never been beyond the ground floor in his house.

On my way up, I spotted a huge collection of family photographs lining the walls of the staircase in apparent date order. The black-and-white ones towards the bottom showed Robert's parents, and what I presumed to be his late wife's. Colour photos supplanted the monochrome for subsequent generations. Robert's wedding photo, taken in front of what looked like a cathedral rather than a parish church, came next. Much as I wanted to know more about my neighbour and his relationship with his late wife, this was completely the wrong time to be nosy. Even so, towards the top of the stairs, I couldn't help but admire a series of beautiful shots of Tilly as a baby and as a toddler, followed by official school photos of her with varying quantities of teeth. Even when her small jaw was full of gaps, she was still adorable. Wherever she was now – perhaps still in that green sports car on her way to goodness knew where – I hoped with all my heart that she was safe.

The playroom must have been a servant's bedroom when

the house was first built, probably furnished with sparse, basic furniture, such as a brass bedstead and marble-topped washstand, built for function rather than comfort. Now it was a little girl's delight, with Flower Fairy curtains, sugar-pink, deep-pile carpet, a four-storey dolls' house, an antique rocking horse, and a whole village of Sylvanians laid out on a playmat printed with lanes, fields and a river.

A vintage-style, open-topped, double-decker omnibus was passing through this Sylvanian village. On the lower deck were tiny dogs and rabbits, but the top deck was occupied by a less likely family: the black king, black queen and two black pawns from Steven's Isle of Lewis chess set. I could understand their appeal to Tilly: they would have fitted as comfortably in her small hands as the familiar Sylvanian animals.

Tucking the whole omnibus under my arm, I hurried down the two flights of stairs back to the sitting room, not wanting to miss anything that the police had to say. I hoped they had promising news.

Unfortunately, they could shed no light on the kidnapping. All they were doing was taking information from Robert and Belinda, rather than reporting progress.

I set the bus on the coffee table. The shorter policeman, who in my absence had donned a pair of clear plastic gloves, held up his hand to stop me removing the Lewis foursome from the upper deck. I presumed he'd want to take them back to the station for fingerprinting. He set them in their rightful places on the chessboard and counted out the pieces.

'So, ten missing in all,' he concluded. 'Why didn't they take them all when they had the chance on Saturday? Half a chess set is about as useful as half a motorbike.'

'Who cares?' Belinda's voice was small but piercing. 'I

don't care if I never see a chess set again. I just want my daughter back.'

Robert, sitting next to her, took one of her hands with both of his and held it tight.

The senior officer turned to me. 'I gather the chess set belongs to you, madam.'

I gave a slight nod. 'Well. I'm kind of minding it for someone: the collector who has asked me to sell his collection of chess sets for him. But I'm sure the owner wouldn't mind if I were to give the remains of this set away to get Tilly back. It's worth very little in any case, in monetary terms, as the wife of the late previous owner confirmed to me when I spoke to her on the phone yesterday. They're nothing compared to a child's life.'

I was surprised they didn't grill me about my phone call to Queenie, but I bowed to their experience.

'Thank you, madam. Then I think the sensible next step is to take this rather unusual ransom note at face value and facilitate the exchange without delay.'

'The ransom note says, "no fuzz",' Robert reminded him. 'Sorry, those are the kidnappers' words, not mine. Are you happy to let us make the exchange without supervision? They've asked for us to meet them in the churchyard at 2 a.m. tonight. So at least it's not long to wait.'

'Oh, we'll be there, right enough. Our presence is essential to protect you, as well as to recover Tilly safely and arrest her abductors. But don't worry, they won't be able to see us.'

'Don't tell me the Gloucestershire Constabulary has powers of invisibility?' mused Belinda.

Robert patted her knee to reprimand her sarcasm, and the police just smiled politely as if she had been making a joke.

'There is a bell tower in your parish church, is there not?' the senior officer continued.

We all nodded.

'With louvred windows to send the sound up and across the village?'

I blinked in surprise. Where was he heading? The second officer, seeing my bewilderment, jabbed his thumb towards his colleague.

'Patrick here is a bell ringer,' he explained. 'Mad about it, he is. Rung in every tower in the county and beyond. Can recite the names and weights of every church bell in Gloucestershire.'

'I've climbed to every bell chamber too,' the other said proudly. 'And let me tell you, if you pull the louvres to a different angle, they make the perfect look-out for anything going on in the vicinity. Three-hundred-and-sixty-degree vision, if required. And the angle of elevation of anyone standing on the ground means they can't see you.'

Robert turned to me. 'I guess the kidnappers assume no one will be about to witness the exchange at that hour.'

'Certainly not in the churchyard,' added Belinda. 'There's too much superstition in sleepy Little Pride for any of its locals to risk strolling among the graves after dark.'

'But what if the kidnapper is already staking the place out?' I asked. 'Won't they run a mile if they see a pair of uniformed police entering the church?'

Patrick beamed. 'But they won't recognise us as police. Let me outline my plan. Nigel and I will join the Little Pride band of ringers for their practice session tonight. Practice nights are 7.30 p.m. until 9 p.m. When the rest of them leave at 9 p.m., we'll stay behind. We'll be in the bell ringers' uniform sweatshirts, and there's enough ringers in the Little Pride band that a couple of extras won't be noticed. I very much doubt the kidnappers will be there early enough to count us in and count us out. But just in case, we've arranged for the band's tower captain to lock the church after the last of them have left, to make it look as if the place is deserted. But I'll borrow a spare set of keys from the church warden, so we can let ourselves out at the strategic moment. I'll keep watch up top and tip off Nigel, who'll stay downstairs by the north porch door, so he can rush out the minute he needs to apprehend the culprit.'

'Supposing there's a gang of them?' asked Belinda sharply. 'A whole gang of villains with guns and knives and smoke cannisters? I don't think Nigel could handle that on his own, or even with you in tow if you ran down the stairs to join him.'

Patrick wagged his finger at her. 'Don't you worry, madam, we'll have reinforcements hiding in the fields behind the church. We won't take any needless risks.'

Belinda folded her arms across her chest and crossed her legs, almost trapping Robert's hand on her knee before he pulled it away.

'I should hope not,' she murmured.

'Who's going to make the exchange, if not the police?' I enquired.

Robert raised his hand.

'The note asked for me,' he reminded us.

My heart did a backflip. Supposing they wanted to take Robert in exchange for Tilly? What if this was all a hoax, designed to lead billionaire Robert into the kidnappers' clutches instead? Anyone rustling Robert could easily demand millions of pounds for his release, confident that his multinational company would pay up. That would make far more sense than abducting his granddaughter for the sake of a few worthless plastic chess pieces. Perhaps Tilly was the proverbial sprat to catch the mackerel. Or rather, Bob Sponge.

'So, what happens now?' asked Belinda, tapping a foot impatiently.

'I suggest you all try to rest as much as you can,' said Patrick. 'Eat your tea and wait for the witching hour.'

I took it that Patrick, like Belinda, was poking fun at the villagers' superstitions.

'Then I'm going home to change,' said Belinda. 'I don't want to be traipsing about a churchyard in the middle of the night in my favourite Manolos. Pa, I'll be back here at midnight in leisurewear.'

'You mustn't come to the churchyard,' said Robert. 'The kidnappers specifically requested me, not you. We can't do anything to jeopardise the exchange. But you're welcome to wait for us here.'

I was glad he'd said that. I wasn't sure Belinda would be able to control herself if she came too, and we didn't want her upsetting the kidnappers with an acerbic comment.

'Oh, and they asked for Alice too,' he added, with an apologetic glance at me.

'Alice. *Alice?*' Belinda was aghast.

'As guardian of the chess set,' he explained. 'They want her to be there too, presumably to assure them they are getting the right goods.'

Startled at the news that I'd be taking part in a potentially dangerous hostage exchange, I tried to distract myself from worrying by packing away the chess pieces. After sweeping them off the coffee table into their box, I snapped it closed and fastened the brass hook and eye to hold it shut.

'Will your husband come back with you tonight?' I asked

Belinda. The more people on our side, the merrier, I reasoned, even if the police insisted that only Robert and I should come to the churchyard.

'No, he's away on business in the Far East.'

She sniffed. Now wasn't the moment to ask the nature of his business.

'If you'd like company while you wait, I'm sure Danny would be happy to sit with you,' I offered.

'Danny lives with Alice,' Robert explained. 'He's a big, strong chap, pleasant enough. You'll like him.'

'Thank you, Alice, I would very much appreciate his company, if you're sure you don't mind.'

I was bemused at her implication that Danny might need my permission to go out. Did her husband operate under similar constraints?

I picked up the chessboard, hugging it close to my chest now that I realised it was in essence worth the same as Tilly – a bizarre conversion rate.

'Then I'll be off, if that's OK?' I said. 'I've left Mum in charge of my shop, and she'll be getting anxious. Shall I come back at about 1.30 a.m., Robert, so we can walk up to the churchyard together?'

I may not have shared the locals' fear of the haunted churchyard, but nor was I about to volunteer to enter it alone with a kidnapper in the vicinity, even with the police watching from the church tower.

'That would be great, Alice, thank you,' said Robert. 'In the meantime, my daughter and I will try to distract ourselves by doing something absorbing and constructive. Belinda, I thought perhaps I might come back to yours and help you arrange your bookshelves in rainbow order. I know you've been planning to do that for a while.'

He knew his daughter so well. She even smiled at the prospect.

'Great, that'll do for tomorrow's Instagram,' she replied.

The policemen, slipping their tablets into capacious tunic pockets, accompanied me to the door.

'And we'll be off to chat up the tower captain and wheedle some spare sweatshirts from him,' said Patrick. 'We'll see you later, Alice, although by the time you see us, little Tilly should be safely back in the arms of her family.'

I so wanted to believe him.

31

THE KITCHEN DETECTIVES

Conscious that Robert was about to leave his house empty, I'd brought the ransom chess set home. Now I couldn't bear to let it out of my sight. I opened the case and spread the pieces out on the kitchen table, where Mum was busy chopping carrots and onions to make a casserole for our tea.

When I filled her in on the police officers' timetable for the evening, her eyes widened with excitement. I was surprised she didn't object to my involvement. Whether this was because she welcomed the implied closeness between Robert and me, or whether because she was of a generation that put complete faith in the police force, I was unsure.

As we talked, I couldn't help fidgeting with the chess pieces, lining them up as if in family or friendship groups, as Tilly had done. I mused at the Sylvanian villagers' charming acceptance of these immigrants who looked so very different from the rest of them.

As Mum was frying the onions in a little olive oil, I heard the shop door open and close and the click of the lock. Remembering the recent intruder, I held my breath. The kidnappers must know where I lived, as the name and address of Alice's Cotswold Curiosity Shop had been all over the publicity for the Chessmates launch event. Supposing they'd been covertly watching my shop and had seen me bring the chess set back to my cottage? What if they decided to pre-empt the evening's plan and accost me for it here instead? My mind worked overtime, planning how to defend Mum with the vegetable knife in one hand and the chopping board in the other. Maybe I could scatter bits of onion across the floor to make the intruders lose their footing.

Then Danny's familiar evening greeting rang out – an ironic, American-style, 'Hi, honey, I'm home.'

'Danny! It's you! Hurrah!'

As he entered the kitchen, the look of relief on my face made him give me a funny look. I wasn't usually quite that welcoming.

'You OK?' he asked, brow furrowed.

'She's not what I call OK,' put in Mum, returning from the cooker to her seat by the table. 'It's all kicking off next door.'

Her tone was light-hearted, but there was a tremor in her voice. I realised she'd been putting on a brave face, which she was now having trouble sustaining.

'Tell him, Alice,' she added, 'while I make us all a nice cup of tea.'

While Mum brewed up, I brought an astonished Danny up to speed. He kindly agreed to sit with Belinda next door while Robert and I obeyed the kidnappers' instructions at the churchyard.

'I'm coming with you, Danny,' said Mum. 'I don't fancy staying here on my own while there are kidnappers at large.'

'I was just about to suggest that,' said Danny. 'I wouldn't have considered abandoning you for a moment.'

In contemplative silence, Danny and I began to drink our tea, while Mum continued to prepare the casserole. Neither of us noticed her pick up an Isle of Lewis bishop, mistaking it for my small, marble pepper grinder, and take it to the stove, where she'd just added browned chicken to the onions and carrots in a casserole dish.

'Oh, for goodness' sake!' she muttered, when the bishop refused to dispense any pepper, no matter how hard she twisted his head. Only when she bashed his mitre against the edge of the worktop, saying, 'I reckon some damp's got inside and clogged the holes up,' followed by a piercing shriek, did I turn round to see what the fuss was about.

Mum was standing open-mouthed, holding two pieces of the supposed pepper pot in her hands. The bishop's head, complete with mitre, had come off in her hand to reveal a deep cavity inside the bishop's body.

I leaped from my chair to take the two pieces from her. I was terrified she'd damaged the chess piece beyond repair, jeopardising the deal with Tilly's kidnappers.

'Mum, what on earth are you doing?' I cried.

'Alice, I'm so, so sorry. I didn't have my glasses on, and I thought it was the pepper pot. Do you think if we superglue the parts back together, the kidnappers won't notice the damage?'

I set the two pieces on the kitchen table and waved her concern away, my anger evaporating like a bead of water on a hot stove when a glint of red inside the bishop's body caught my eye.

'Far from it, Mum. In fact, I think you've just singlehand-edly solved the mystery as to why the kidnappers set such great store by this particular chess set.'

With shaking hands, I upended the bishop's body on the

kitchen table and gave it a sharp rap. There was a tiny clatter as out onto the wooden surface rolled a ruby cut in the shape of a torpedo, presumably to allow as big a gemstone as possible to fit inside the cavity. So artfully had it been cut that it was too snug inside the bishop to rattle. It must have been the work of a highly skilled craftsman – and smuggler.

'No wonder Chas King was so angry when Queenie despatched this set to my Steven instead of the other Steven that he'd intended it for. It all makes sense now. Chas's import business was a cover for a gem-smuggling racket, master-minded by Eric Vyse, of which the traces were hidden by selling jewel-filled sets for peanuts on eBay to carefully selected receivers.'

'I'm guessing they also sold normal, cheap sets to mask the illicit trade,' said Danny. 'How odd to use an Isle of Lewis chess set as a cover, though. A set originating on a Scottish island seems an unlikely partner with gemstones that must have originated from far away – India, perhaps.'

'Maybe that's why they chose it,' I considered. 'To be less obvious. Also, the Isle of Lewis chess pieces are much chunkier and more accommodating than, say, the more intri-cate Alice in Wonderland set or the carved elephants. So that's where the export part of Eric and Chas's business came in. Eric sent innocent-looking British reproduction sets to India, where whoever was his local partner-in-crime hollowed them out and inserted stolen gemstones. That would be far less suspicious than a set originally from India. No one's going to expect to find something precious like that inside a plastic replica set.'

'How delighted that Eric Vyse must have been when Queenie gave him her husband's entire stock for free after he died,' said Danny. 'I wonder whether the guy is still trading? Whether we'll find him on eBay?'

'I doubt it,' I said. 'Queenie thinks he's fled to Spain. He's probably recruited another mug to fill the void left by Chas and keeps himself offline. I bet it was him that arranged for Chas to be bumped off in that car accident when Queenie shipped the jewel-filled chess set to the wrong Steven. Lucky he didn't also send his henchmen after Steven to wrestle it off him, but Queenie must have already destroyed the paperwork showing our address by then. And she'd shut down her husband's email and mobile account.'

'Maybe she knew all along what he was up to, and that's why she was hiding the evidence of her involvement – so she wasn't implicated in his crimes,' Danny surmised.

'I thought that you could never really delete anything off the internet or from your computer,' I remarked. 'The police find incriminating evidence on people's computers all the time.'

Mum set the kitchen timer and sat down at the table.

'Well, you pair of Sherlocks,' she began, 'I suggest you let the police know what we've discovered, in case that makes them want to change the procedure for this evening.'

I gazed at her for a moment. Why hadn't I given Mum more credit in this case?

'You're absolutely right, Mum,' I replied. 'Maybe it'll be that Eric Vyse, or one of his henchmen, coming to swap the chess set for Tilly. He's probably already known to the police as a dodgy dealer and illegal smuggler. And now we know the true value of the chess set, the financial stakes are much, much higher. Not that Tilly's safety isn't far more important than any smuggled gemstones.'

Mum picked up another chess piece, this time a knight. 'So do we assume there are jewels inside every one of them?'

When she raised it to shoulder height as if to bash it against the table to find out, I reached out to stay her arm.

'Mum, don't! They might not all come apart as neatly as the bishop. And we don't know yet how easily we can repair it.'

From my writing desk, Nell's old upright bureau, I fetched a tube of superglue that I'd used the previous week to repair a chipped vintage vase.

Danny and Mum watched in silence as I squeezed a tiny ring of glue around the bishop's broken neck and pressed his head back into place. To my relief, I made a passable job of it. Danny picked it up by its base and raised it to the overhead light.

'Well done, Alice, I can't see the join. Better leave it to dry for the moment. In the meantime, why don't you phone the policemen and tell them our discovery?'

I pulled Patrick's card from my pocket and took my mobile into the garden to get a signal. I got through to Patrick straight away and quickly told him the story of the bishop's surprising innards. He listened without a word until I reached the end.

'So, we think Eric Vyse could be the man behind all this,' I concluded. 'With Malcolm Ashby his unfortunate messenger boy. But as we know from the Jorkinses' evidence, Malcolm was in dire financial straits, and I'm guessing he knew what was inside the chess pieces. But I assume Vyse got wind that Ashby was planning to keep them for himself to pay off his debts – or to enable him to gamble even more. Hence another of Vyse's sidekicks turned up in the car park to take them off him. Perhaps they meant only to knock him out as a punishment or a warning, rather than to kill him, while taking the chess pieces off him. But it is what it is.'

Patrick was silent for a moment. 'Why didn't Vyse just send Ashby or some other minion to steal it from your house before the sale?' he asked.

'Actually, I think he might have sent someone to steal the rest of the set from me on Sunday night, because Ashby had only managed to seize eleven pieces.' I recounted to him the incident of my peculiar late-night visitor.

'If you captured his visit on CCTV, we'll be requisitioning the footage,' he said. 'Do you have CCTV?'

I grimaced. 'No, not yet. But I am planning to paint an old biscuit tin in the style of a camera to put on the front wall of the shop.'

Patrick tutted.

'Little Pride!' he said, which for a moment I took for a derisory comment about my self-respect, until I realised it was a general dismissal of the whole village's security standards. He must have known it was common practice around here to put up dummy cameras. 'You lot are in your own little world out there.'

Even though it was hardly a compliment, I found myself flushing with pleasure at being considered part of the community, rather than as a townie incomer.

'But what about this Eric Vyse?' I went on. 'Is he known to the police? I realise Chas King was outside your patch, but aren't all the nation's constabularies linked together on the same computer network?'

'That we are,' replied Patrick. 'And let me reassure you, if we've a trace of this Vyse guy on the national crime database, by the time I come to bell-ringing practice tonight, I'll have his mugshot, fingerprints and criminal record on hand so that we can recognise him in the unlikely event that he turns up to do the dirty work himself. Although we only have Queenie King's word for it that he's holed up somewhere in Spain. Otherwise, tonight's plan continues unchanged.'

I gulped. What other lies might Queenie King have told me?

As the hours ticked away, the action plan was starting to seem frighteningly real – and imbued with danger for us all.

'Perhaps you'd like to pose as a ringer and come up at 7.30 p.m. for practice yourself, so we can fill you in about anything we'd found on Vyse by then?' he suggested. 'We can get the tower captain to drop a spare bell-ringers' sweatshirt off to your house so as not to arouse suspicion.'

I felt obliged to agree.

* * *

As the grandfather clock was striking a quarter past seven, I became aware of a strange echo effect outside and further up the road – a cluster of bells, each sounding a different note, clanging together.

'Ah, that'll be the bell ringers getting ready for practice,' I told Mum. 'Before they can start ringing properly, they have to ring the bells up.'

I was proud of the insight I'd gained into how church bells work, from when one of the ringers had tried to recruit me for their band not long after I'd moved to Little Pride. He'd given me an educational tour of the bell chamber and ringing platform.

'The bells are kept with their mouths facing downwards for safety,' I explained. 'But before they can do change ringing, they have to haul the bells upside down to their required starting point, with the mouths facing upwards. Then each time they pull on the rope, the bell turns a full circle, and the clapper strikes the side of the bell.'

Mum and Danny still looked a bit puzzled, but there was no time now to go into detail. I needed to get to the church.

'Danny, will you walk up with her please?' Mum asked as I shrugged on my coat.

'No, Mum, honestly, I'll be fine,' I protested, glad that Danny would be staying home with Mum to keep her safe. 'It's early evening, and there'll be plenty of people out and about, walking dogs and so forth. There's no need.'

Mum folded her arms across her chest.

'Listen to your mother, Alice.' So she was pulling rank. 'Danny, you go with her.'

I felt about ten years old again, and I bet Danny did too.

'If you insist, Wendy.'

She gave him a beatific smile. 'Thank you, Danny, dear. I'll turn the casserole down when it's done, and we can eat together when the practice session finishes. No need to rush. A casserole always tastes better for the extra time in the oven.'

Danny turned to me, clearly torn.

'Can you get one of the other ringers to walk you home afterwards for safety, Alice?' he asked.

'That's easy enough,' I said. 'Two of them live just down the road from here and will pass my door on their way home. We'll lock the shop on the way out, Mum, and you should bolt the door behind us. Then take the chess set upstairs and barricade yourself in one of the bedrooms. My bedroom if that makes you feel safer. The front bedroom window opens onto the high street, so if you are worried, you can shout out of the window for attention, and neighbours will come running. Otherwise, don't leave the bedroom till you see

Danny arriving back. Then of course you'll have to go down and unbolt the door to let him in.'

'I'll run all the way back from the church, Wendy,' Danny reassured her. 'I won't leave you alone for a second longer than absolutely necessary.'

To my surprise, Mum consented without demur. She was far pluckier than I'd given her credit for, but I suppose neither of us had been in this kind of peril before me to find out. What else had I yet to discover about Mum, now that I was taking the time to get to know her better as an adult? I felt a warm glow on the inside realising how much more we'd connected during the last couple of days, after spending far too long apart.

Mum beamed in gratitude. 'Thank you, my dears. You're good children.'

As Danny and I headed for the door, we exchanged amused glances at her term for us. But there was no doubt about it, spending time with Mum was making me feel much younger – in a good way.

32

DEAD RINGERS

Danny lingered at the foot of the bell tower's spiral staircase just long enough for me to mount the steps and enter the ringing platform, where seven familiar figures from the village, and Patrick, were heaving rhythmically on the bell ropes. Patrick's bell sounded the deepest.

'Two over three.' One of about five bystanders was shouting to be heard above the tolling. 'Now back to rounds.'

Patrick caught sight of me as I closed the arched wooden door to the stairs behind me and raised his eyebrows apologetically. I realised I'd have to wait for a natural break before trying to speak to him. The ringers all wore such looks of concentration that I didn't like to interrupt their flow.

'Stand!' cried the caller at last, and after a couple more pulls from each ringer, the bells fell silent.

Patrick tied his bell rope in a loose knot to stop it trailing on the floor before walking around the outside of the circle of ringers to greet me. One of the bystanders sprang across the chamber to take his place at the spare bell. Nigel, sitting on a chair watching the ringers, got up to join us.

I glanced around, wondering how much the village ringers knew about why Patrick, Nigel and I were there. Supposing Eric Vyse was among them, and was actually a longstanding villager using a pseudonym?

Even so, I didn't want to risk revealing anything that might endanger our mission. When I eyed the door, Patrick raised a hand to attract the attention of the other ringers, now chatting amiably during this break in the ringing.

'Sorry, chaps, Nigel and I just need to step outside for a moment for a quick chat with Alice. Do carry on without us.' He held the door open for me.

'Upstairs or down?' I asked.

Patrick guffawed. 'Downstairs, I think, Alice. If we go upstairs to the bell chamber and they start ringing again, we'll be deafened.'

I descended to the vestry, hanging on to the vertical rope that served as a banister at the centre of the ancient, spiral stone staircase. When Patrick and Nigel had joined me, I spoke in a low voice as I explained Mum's discovery of the ruby.

'Your Eric Vyse,' Patrick began, rubbing his chin in thought. 'Turns out he was involved with a jewel heist many years ago up Milton Keynes way.'

'Did he get sent to prison for his part in the heist?' I said.

'Yes, but that term was spent a while back. It was pretty early in my career, and I remember reading about it in the national press. Seems his time inside did nothing to abate his taste for sparklers, though.' He turned to me. 'Alice, do you have any idea where Queenie King was when you spoke to her?'

'No, but we'll be able to tell from my phone,' I replied. 'Although she hung up when I asked her postal address, I'd called her landline, so the dialling code will give us the general location.'

I pulled out my phone and swiped back through the call history. '01908,' I read from the screen.

Patrick nodded. 'That's Milton Keynes all right.' He gazed at his feet for a moment.

'Is he dangerous, sir?' asked Nigel in a casual tone that I suspect was intended to put me at my ease.

'Let's just say we may need to bring in further reinforcements, as well as the family liaison officer we've got lined up to support Tilly. But, Alice, you and Robert Praed proceed as originally planned. In fact, don't tell Robert what we've discovered. He'll be anxious enough about his granddaughter's safety, and I don't want to frighten him further. Just remember, we've got your backs.'

This was going to demand more courage than I thought I had within me, but remembering how brave Mum was being, I determined to follow her lead. Besides, if all else failed, thinking of those pictures of little Tilly on Robert's stairs would keep me going. I may not have been lucky enough to have children of my own, but I could still feel inherent maternal instincts. I was determined to make sure that Tilly would still be around to add her secondary school photos to the gallery on Robert's staircase.

33

TOWERING VICTORY

By the time I arrived home, escorted to my front door by the two amiable old ringers who lived further down the high street, I was so full of adrenaline that I could barely bring myself to sit down. While Danny turned on the television, seeking something to pass the time and take our minds off what lay ahead, Mum picked up her knitting bag and drew out her latest project: red poppies ready for Remembrance Day in a few weeks' time, which she was making to raise funds for the Royal British Legion.

Watching me pace the room, hugging myself for comfort, she reached into her bag and pulled out a spare ball of scarlet yarn.

'Here, dear, fetch a pair of number eights and I'll tell you how to knit a poppy.'

It was just what I needed – a little mindfulness, requiring me to concentrate on an unfamiliar pattern while the clock ticked the night away. The rhythmic clicking of the needles and the familiar feel of the soft yarn slipping through my fingers was just the therapy I needed. Ignoring the television,

Mum started chatting to me about making knitted items to sell in my shop. Then I got down my collection of knitting pattern books, and we spent a pleasant hour browsing through them. Mum even volunteered to make as many things as I could sell in my shop and send them to me by post.

'I don't really have anyone to knit garments for these days,' she said, staring at her needles. 'Not since you grew too fashion-conscious to want home-made jumpers. And now I'm without Dad...'

I blinked as tears welled up in my eyes and pretended to focus on my knitting.

'I don't mind paying the postage,' she added, as if that might have been a reason for me to reject her very kind offer.

I thought quickly. 'I tell you what, Mum. Why don't you knit a batch of seasonal things as the year goes by, and bring them across in person every few months? You can help me set them out in the shop and display them nicely. You might even sit in the shop and do some knitting demonstrations during your stays. You've always been such a good craft teacher.'

Mum's face flushed with pleasure.

'If you're sure, dear.' She didn't need any more encouragement. 'I could teach any interested customers to knit too, if you like,' she continued. 'Not that I want to make myself redundant. I'll always be happy to knit for you, for as long as you want me to.'

I smiled. 'You'll never be redundant, Mum. Not while I'm around.'

I put down my half-finished poppy and crossed to her armchair to give her a hug. Before I could straighten up, she kissed the top of my head, as she used to do when I was little after tucking me in at night and turning on my nightlight in the shape of a fairy castle.

'Let me make us another cup of tea,' I added, before dashing out into the kitchen to surreptitiously dry my eyes.

I just hoped that I'd still be here for her, and Tilly for Belinda, after the night was over.

* * *

At about a quarter past one, there was a gentle tap at the front door.

'That'll be Robert come to call for me,' I said, getting up to slip on the puffer jacket that I had left at the ready on the back of the sofa.

Ever vigilant, Danny put his hand up to stop me while he went to the door to check.

It was indeed Robert. With my coat on, I slid the Isle of Lewis chess set into a canvas messenger bag and passed the strap over my neck to make sure no one could grab it from me and run off, without taking me with it.

I roused Mum from her doze on the sofa. She had refused to go to bed until we had accomplished our rescue mission. Once she'd put on her coat and shoes, she and Danny followed us as far as Robert's front gate. We could see Belinda standing in the lounge window, clutching a crystal glass of some spirit with both hands. I gave her a wave and a thumbs-up sign, and Robert blew her a kiss, as Danny opened the gate to admit Mum in front of him. Only when Belinda had opened the door, and Danny and Mum had gone safely inside and bolted it behind them, did Robert and I continue up the high street to the church.

There was only a sliver of moon above, partly shrouded by a misty ring that promised frost before dawn, but my shivering was not caused by the cold. Instinctively, I looped my arm through Robert's as we strode past the pub, leaning in close to be comforted by his body warmth. He turned to look at me, raising his eyebrows in surprise.

'Good thing Danny's watching your mum and not you,' he said lightly, one corner of his mouth turning up in a bemused half-smile.

'Why, do you think she's in more danger than I am?'

Robert gave a muffled laugh, perhaps trying not to wake the sleeping villagers whose cottages we were strolling past – not a single one was burning a light – or to avoid giving away our whereabouts to the waiting kidnapper before we reached the churchyard.

He raised the crooked right elbow in which my left hand was nestling.

'Actually, I meant I didn't want to make him jealous.' He patted my left hand with his own for emphasis.

'Jealous? Danny?' When my voice rose to a squeak, he put a finger to his lips to hush me. I resorted to a whisper. 'But Danny's only my lodger. We're just friends. You didn't think...?'

'Oh!' exclaimed Robert, and it was my turn to shush him. 'But I've heard how he greets you when he gets home from work. And seen you close – and other stuff.'

I shook my head vigorously. 'We're just friends. I've only offered him my spare room as a temporary solution after he left his ex-boyfriend in a hurry after being let down by him.'

'Oh!' said Robert again. 'His ex-boyfriend. Oh.'

I passed my hand over my eyes, momentarily giddy. Of all the times to have this enlightening conversation, this was hardly ideal. I'd have liked nothing more than to pursue this discussion, but for now, just seeing the light in his eyes that showed he was interested in me after all was enough to sustain me until a more appropriate occasion to strike up a romantic relationship – ideally by candlelight over a bottle of good wine in his elegant lounge.

Just then, the sound of a motorbike reached us from beyond the churchyard. Perhaps one of Jack Dauntless's biker friends was involved after all?

The damp night air had wound wreaths of fog about the dense, dark yew trees edging the churchyard, and small clouds drifted about the gravestones beyond. I took my arm from Robert's as we broke into a run.

The engine noise dropped slightly as the biker turned into the small car park beside the church. As we saw him pass the empty spaces and head for the lychgate, we could just about make out a dark, squarish shape on the seat behind him. He lifted the latch and nudged the gate open with his front wheel, before driving through and up the gravel path and around the foot of the bell tower into the churchyard.

'He looked quite stocky,' I hissed as we neared the open lychgate, suddenly conscious of Robert's age. 'He might be really powerful. Don't cross him, will you?'

'If he was that sturdy a chap, he'd have needed a bigger bike,' he returned. 'That was never the engine noise of some tough Hells Angel's wheels – more like a kid's motor scooter.'

Not knowing enough about the difference between motorbikes and scooters to judge, I took Robert's word for it.

'Anyway, I don't think that bulk was all him. I think he had something like a pizza delivery bag on his back. Delivering small children a sideline.'

Impressed by his ability to joke at such a tense time, I followed him through the lychgate and up the path towards the church. Stopping outside the west porch at the bottom of the tower, we realised the biker had turned his vehicle round to point straight at us. Was he making ready for a quick getaway – or did he plan to mow us down?

I glanced up at the top of the tower to reassure myself that the police did indeed have our backs. I couldn't see Patrick, but I did notice the wooden louvred shutters had been opened at a different angle since bell-ringing practice, to allow Patrick a good view of the ground while remaining hidden himself.

No one had spoken since we'd entered the churchyard. Taking the initiative, I opened my messenger bag and took out the first chess piece that came to hand – a white knight clutching a shield and riding its own little chunky horse. I held it up between thumb and forefinger, the knight facing the biker as if the two of them were about to ride towards each other in some kind of surreal jousting match.

'I have all the remaining pieces of the Isle of Lewis chess set in this bag.' My voice rang out across the deserted churchyard, seeming to bounce off the ancient, crooked gravestones. 'I presume you, or an accomplice, have the rest, which you stole from Malcolm Ashby in the school car park. Which he had stolen from us. But never mind that now. Please just give us Tilly. Where are you hiding her?'

The biker took his hands off his handlebars for a moment to reach over his shoulders to remove the pizza delivery bag and sling it onto the gravel. Whichever firm he worked for, they must have served very generous-sized pizzas. But as it fell almost noiselessly to the ground, I realised it was empty.

'Come on, Tilly,' he hissed over his shoulder.

Then I realised that at his waist were two small hands in dark mittens, almost invisible against his black leather jacket, apart from a small, white, Hello Kitty logo on each one.

All of a sudden, a familiar face popped out from behind his right arm.

'Surprise!' cried Tilly, all smiles.

She must have been hidden under the open, upended pizza delivery bag on the seat behind him. From her cheery manner, she seemed to be treating this whole escapade as a fun game. In a way, that was no bad thing – at least she should be less traumatised than if she'd been terrified the whole time.

'Tilly!' Robert was about to run to her, but the biker held up one hand to stop him, and with the other, revved his engine.

'Not until you give me your bag,' he insisted in a surprisingly high voice. 'Fair do's.'

The s was lisped.

'I'll give you fair—' began Robert, taking a step forward and raising his fists.

I grabbed the hem of Robert's jacket to drag him back before he could do anything rash that might endanger Tilly. The adrenaline surging through me made me so strong that I almost pulled Robert off his feet. And I no longer feared the biker, because I now knew who it was.

As Robert staggered to regain his balance, I whipped off my messenger bag and rushed forward to loop it over the biker's neck, felling them like I'd thrown a ring over the stick on a fairground hoopla stall. But my prize was no goldfish. It was Tilly, who I scooped up into my arms and hugged to my chest with as much passion as if she'd been my own child.

Robert dashed to my side to take her from me as the biker, apparently thinking the deal was done and our business completed, threaded one arm through the webbing strap of the messenger bag and positioned it comfortably on their back.

But before they could drive off, I launched a karate-style kick to send the motor scooter toppling sideways onto the grassy bank beside the gravel path, trapping its rider underneath.

'What the—?' cried the biker.

Just then, the lychgate slammed shut, thanks to a dark rope that we'd not noticed before, yanked from somewhere amid the yews.

'Not so fast, my lad,' cried Nigel, stepping out from among the greenery in full camouflage gear.

'Actually, it's my girl,' I replied. 'Or rather, woman. And her name is Queenie King. At least, I think it is. Or it's one of the names she goes by.'

Before I could explain further, the chill air was rent by deep reverberations of the tenor bell – the deepest bell of the right of eight – chiming over and over again. As if at a signal, half a dozen police officers in anti-riot gear charged out from all around us – from behind trees and gravestones, and even from within a freshly dug open grave. They all headed for the felled biker. I realised the tolling of the church bell had been to alert the police officers to attend the scene.

One of them raised the bike and propped it up on its kick-stand, and two more dragged its rider upright while a fourth flipped up the visor on the rider's helmet.

Robert lifted Tilly up and held her against his chest so that she was facing away from the action, whispering reassurances in her ear. He had to whisper them quite loudly to be heard above the chiming bell.

Then, as suddenly as it had started, the bell's chiming

ceased, the absence of its clanging making the air feel far stiller than before it had begun.

As one of the officers was arresting the rider on suspicion of abduction and reading her rights, the great door at the foot of the tower flew open, and Patrick appeared, slightly out of breath from running down the spiral stairs straight after such a strenuous bout of tolling the heaviest bell. As soon as Patrick caught sight of Queenie's unmistakeably female face, complete with dark ticks of eyeliner, thick mascara and sugar-pink lipstick, he did a double take, but not for the reason I was expecting.

'Pearl Pigeon, as I live and breathe!' he cried. 'A couple of decades older than the last picture we have on file of you, but unmistakeably you. I'd recognise that shade of lippy anywhere.'

Pearl Pigeon – or Queenie King, or whoever she'd decided to be today – tried to take a step back in alarm, but the secure grip of the two officers either side of her ensured she could go nowhere without their permission.

'How do you know who I am?' she asked.

'Because when I was not much older than you, your old flame Eric Vyse pulled off the famous Milton Keynes jewellery heist. It was the excitement of that case in the daily papers that made me decide to join the force. I couldn't read enough about it. I could go on *Mastermind*, I could, with Milton Keynes Jewellery Heist as my special subject. So, what you are up to, Pearl? Running little errands to earn your flight out to join him in Spain, are you?'

When Patrick turned a penlight torch on Pearl's face, she bridled – and I gasped aloud, recognising a remarkable similarity to the night-time intruder in my shop.

'You got nothing on me, mate,' she retorted. 'All I'm doing is bringing this little lost girl back home. Can't a lady do a good turn now and again without the law coming down on her?'

Patrick snorted. 'Little lost girl, my eye! If this is meant to be a mercy errand, how come you're bringing the child to a deserted graveyard at two o'clock in the morning, and not delivering her to the doorstep of her family home? Don't give me that nonsense, Pearl Pigeon. And what did you think this bag was for that this lady's just kindly given you, eh?' He wrenched it off her and held it tauntingly at arm's length, just out of her reach. 'A tasty picnic to keep your strength up on the way home to Milton Keynes?'

As Pearl's shoulders slumped, Patrick's tone changed from a playful wheedling to a harsh bark. 'And was it you that despatched another fellow on two wheels in the school car park on Saturday?'

'Gives a whole new meaning to the term "despatch rider", sir,' said Nigel, grimacing.

The woman scowled. 'You mean Malcolm Ashby? My boy Jimmy was only getting back what was rightfully my Eric's.'

'Your Eric's?' I blurted. 'I thought your husband was Chas?'

I guessed Chas's death had led to a romantic reunion with her old flame Eric.

'Yes,' she said. 'What's his is mine and what's mine's me own. It was Eric's originally, and Chas was trading it for him.'

'Laundering,' Patrick corrected her. 'Smuggling illegally imported, stolen gems.'

'Anyway, we'd seen the set on a chess group page on Facebook, and I recognised it at once as one that was rightly ours.

It was meant to be Chas's retirement fund. Then when Chas got done in, I decided to try to get it back to fund a new life in Spain for me. So, I paid Malcolm Ashby a good price to collect the pieces from the sale at the school. He went with cash in his pocket to buy them, but when he found out they weren't for sale, he had to resort to pocketing them instead. Fair do's. Then my boy Jimmy was to collect them from him in the local pub. My Jimmy didn't want to be seen inside the school hisself, just in case there was security cameras about because, well, reasons. But when the time came, Malcolm only gave Jimmy a handful of pieces, and said he couldn't take no more because some woman had rumbled him and he had to make a dash for it. Malcolm Ashby's always been a lying toad, so of course my Jimmy didn't believe him. Fair do's. So my Jimmy walloped him in the car park, and Malcolm just slid to the floor, like the useless lump he is. It's not my Jimmy's fault that Malcolm's head wasn't up to much.'

'It certainly isn't now,' said Patrick drily.

'But once Jimmy had searched Malcolm, he realised he really didn't have the rest of the pieces. He reasoned you must have taken the remainder back to your stupid junk shop.'

'Curiosity Shop, please,' I corrected her, but she just shrugged it off.

'So, I sent Jim to your shop the next night to look for the rest. Even then he couldn't find them. Honestly, kids these days, if you want something done properly, you have to do it yourself.'

I realised it was time to tell my side of that story.

'Officers, I believe Jimmy broke into my shop on Sunday night with malicious intent, but I frightened him off and he left empty-handed.'

Perhaps I'd tell the police later that Jimmy had entered the shop through an unlocked door, but I didn't want to tell that to Pearl/Queenie.

Queenie continued as if I hadn't spoken.

'So that's why I've had to resort to doing this swap – the rest of the set for this little girl.' She gazed around defiantly, as if she was only doing what any sensible, logical, responsible adult would do. 'And that was a piece of cake. I knew you had this rich neighbour, and all I had to do was hire a car the dead spit of his, and pick her up from school at home-time. I thought a middle-aged woman like you would be a sucker for a kidnapped child story.'

'Excuse me!' I cried. 'I'm not middle-aged! I'm only fifty!'

She gave me a withering look before turning to Patrick. 'Here, Alice Carroll's the one you should be nicking, not me. Arrest her for handling stolen goods! That chess set was never rightfully hers.'

I put my hands on my hips. 'How dare you! We didn't know they were stolen. My friend bought that set off your husband fair and square via eBay, and I've got the receipt to prove it. Thirty quid he paid for it. It's not his fault you sent him the wrong set, the one loaded up with secret gemstones you were trying to launder over eBay. It was due to your incompetence. You told me as much the other day when I phoned you.'

She turned her head away, nose in the air. 'Don't believe her, Officers; she's no proof we've ever spoken.'

I didn't miss a beat.

'I recorded the call,' I snapped.

Goodness, I really was getting good at telling lies these days.

Her face fell, and her whole body went limp in defeat.

As Patrick gestured to the officers restraining her to start walking, a police van appeared in the car park, headlights illuminating the churchyard and the yews like some spooky laser show.

'Come on, lads, let's take her away. Nigel, you can do the honours.'

'But what about my bike?' Pearl whined. 'I borrowed it off my boy, and Jimmy will do his nut if he doesn't get it back by morning.'

'Neither of you will be needing a bike of any shape or size where you're going,' said Patrick calmly. 'But look on the bright side. You'll both have plenty of time inside to master the wonderful game of chess, provided you keep your nose clean and don't end up in solitary. One-sided chess isn't half so much fun.'

We watched in silence as the two officers escorted Pearl to the police van.

A second car drew up, and a woman of about forty in civilian clothes stepped out of the rear passenger door and came to join us.

Patrick turned to Robert. 'Usually in such cases, we'd take the child with us to be debriefed by my colleague Delia here, who is a specially trained officer for such matters, but as Tilly has been gone such a short time, and she seems in good spirits, perhaps you'd prefer to take her home now, sir, and call our officer for support in your own time?'

Robert nodded as Delia handed him her business card. 'Yes, I think what's best for all concerned right now is to reunite her with her mother. She's waiting at my house. I'm hoping they'll both be sleeping over at mine tonight.'

Tilly raised her head from Robert's chest. 'Can I play with my Sylvanian omnibus before I have to go to bed?'

Robert's lips twitched in amusement. 'Ask your mother when we get home.'

Meanwhile, Nigel had righted the motor scooter and rescued the helmet from the path.

'Would you like me to drive it back to the station, sir?' he enquired of Patrick, sounding hopeful. 'I'll take it careful, and I'll wear her helmet.'

'All right, son, if you must,' said Patrick. 'There shouldn't be many coppers about at this time of night, anyway.'

He grinned as Nigel tootled off down the high street at an entirely legal twenty miles per hour. Then he turned back to Robert and me. 'Shall I run you home, sir, madam, miss? My car's at your disposal if you wish.'

Robert was still hugging Tilly, who was clinging to him like a baby koala to its mother. He shook his head. 'Thank you, Officer, but I think we'll be happy to walk home. The fresh air will clear our heads, and walking will calm us all down. A dose of normality is what we could all do with right now. But thank you for all you've done. I can never thank you enough.'

Patrick smiled, a twinkle in his eye. 'I'll remember your words when it's time to start selling tickets for the policemen's ball.'

Conscious that there was something missing, I swung around, trying to think what it might be. Of course! The messenger bag!

'Don't worry, Alice,' said Patrick, placing a firm hand on the familiar bag that now hung across his body. 'We'll keep this safe down at the station. All in good time, we will return the smuggled jewels to their rightful owners, and the chess set to your good self, if, as I expect, it turns out that your friend acquired it legally and innocently.'

'I assure you he did,' I said earnestly. 'I wouldn't mind the bag back, but feel free to keep the chess set to use at the station in your coffee breaks, once the case is over,' I said. 'I think we'll stick to Sylvanians in future, shall we, Tilly?'

But Tilly was already fast asleep in Robert's arms.

34

BACK IN THEIR BOX

As Robert and I wandered quietly back down the high street, we hadn't expected to see any signs of life. To our surprise, quite a few cottages now had lights turned on, and a few clusters of neighbours were chattering over party walls and on doorsteps.

'Oi, Bob Sponge!' A quavering voice cut through the chill night air. 'What's going on? Has there been an invasion?'

Robert and I exchanged puzzled glances.

'No,' he replied to Maudie Frampton, who had trudged up her front path to the garden gate in her huge carpet slippers. 'Why, were you expecting one?'

Robert turned to me.

'During the last war, the bells were silent for the duration, only to be tolled to signal the Nazis were coming, which never happened, of course.'

'Well, you never know these days,' Maudie returned. 'What with that funny fellow with the hair in America and the Russian who keeps taking his shirt off.'

'Ah, international politics in a nutshell,' murmured

Robert so that only I should hear. Then he raised his voice to reply to Maudie. 'Nothing to worry about, Mrs Frampton, just a little police exercise. You can read all about it in next month's *Little Pride Parish News*.'

I hid a gratified smile.

'We in Little Pride can all sleep safely in our beds tonight.'

Maudie, reluctant to be so easily mollified, pointed an accusing finger at the recumbent Tilly.

'Which is exactly where that babby should be. What are you thinking of, dragging her about the village at this time of night? She should be tucked up in bed.'

'Don't worry, Maudie, that's exactly where I'm taking her right now.'

Before I could stop myself, I thought, *I wish you'd do the same for me*.

But I had to make do with just looping my hand through the crook of his elbow, where it nestled in a snug spot between his coat sleeve and Tilly's little leg.

'Tilly, darling,' said Robert, as we neared home. 'Tell me one thing, and I promise I won't be cross with you. You do know not to go off with strangers, don't you? Mummy and Daddy have told you lots of times never to get into the car of a person you don't know. So why did you go off with that lady you didn't know?'

Tilly pulled back from his arms, pushing her hands against his chest so that she could look him in the eye.

'Because she was driving your car, and she told me she was going to be my new grandma. I've been telling Mummy for ages that I'd like a new grandma. This lady told me you'd sent her to pick me up in your car so I could get to know her better. It made perfect sense to me.'

Her little face, pale in the moonlight and from lack of

sleep, crumpled as she realised her error. 'But she's not, is she? She told me a great big fib.'

'No, darling,' said Robert gently. 'But everything's fine and you're safe now, so no need to worry. I told you I wouldn't be cross.'

Tilly sighed. 'I would still quite like a new grandma, though. All my friends have got two, and I've only got Daddy's mummy. I told Mummy I thought Alice would make a good grandma. What do you think?'

I pulled my hand away from Robert's arm and covered my face with both hands in embarrassment. No wonder Belinda had been a little cool towards me. I hope she didn't think I'd put Tilly up to this request.

Robert, diplomatic as ever, replied calmly, 'Alice would be very good at all sorts of things. But no one can just place orders for new grandmas, like Mummy orders groceries from Ocado.'

'That's a pity,' said Tilly, wrapping her arms about his neck and snuggling up against his chest again.

Before Robert could reply, she had fallen back to sleep.

* * *

When we reached Robert's house, the light in the lounge was still blazing, the curtains wide open, presumably so that Belinda could catch sight of Tilly the moment she arrived. Danny opened the front door as we reached it, and Mum, peering out from behind him, pushed him aside with surprising force to run towards me.

'Alice, my Alice! You're safe!'

My mouth fell open in surprise. Surely Tilly and Belinda were the ones meant to be having the dramatic reunion?

Then I surrendered, hugging her back with all the strength I had left.

'I'm very glad to see you too, Mum.'

By the time we stood apart, Robert had already transferred the somnolent Tilly onto Belinda's lap without waking her. When Mum, Danny and I entered the lounge, Mum and I holding hands, Belinda was shedding silent, happy tears, rocking her little girl on her lap. Robert picked up a tartan cashmere throw from a nearby basket and draped it over them.

'I think you'd better stay the night, love,' he said to his daughter gently. 'That little girl has had more than enough excitement for one night, and you'll both get more rest if you put her down here now than if you have to wake her up to drive her home.'

'Thanks, Daddy, I'd like that,' said Belinda, squeezing the hand he'd gently laid on her shoulder.

Mum hovered near the doorway. 'Robert, can I make you all a hot drink now? You and Alice must be chilled through, hanging around a graveyard at this time of night.'

Robert was looking thoughtfully at Danny, as if still processing what he'd learned about him earlier that evening.

'Don't feel obliged, Wendy, but thanks for offering. You take Alice and Danny home and take care of yourselves. Belinda, Tilly and I will be fine now.'

Mum reached up to give Robert a peck on the cheek on her way to the door.

'Thank you for looking after my little girl too,' she said, suddenly sounding old.

'Thank you for helping to solve the mystery, Wendy, by uncovering the jewels hidden inside the chess set,' he said with a little bow of homage.

Mum brightened. 'Yes, I suppose I did, didn't I?'

As we walked down the path to the gate, she whispered to me, 'Such a nice man.'

At the gate, Robert reached out to shake Danny's hand. 'Thanks for being Belinda's guard dog tonight.'

Danny grinned. 'Any time, Robert. Although I have to say this whole business has put me right off chess.'

I frowned. 'Does that mean you'll withdraw from Chessmates?'

'Oh no,' said Danny quickly. 'Not now I've promised Jack Dauntless.'

A smile spread slowly across my face. I thought he and Jack had been having an extraordinary number of planning meetings without me, and now I realised the truth. But Danny knew me too well for my reaction to pass him by. He scratched his nose.

'Oops! Have I just blown my cover?'

I laughed. 'Don't worry, Danny, I'm just glad you're back in the game.'

He laid an affectionate hand on my shoulder as I unlocked my front door. 'I suppose I am. So, Alice, when will it be your turn?'

I grinned as I crossed the threshold. 'Actually, I just played my opening gambit with Robert on the way to the churchyard tonight.'

35

END GAME

Ever since I took over as editor of the *Little Pride Parish News*, I'd been concerned that I might not be able to rustle up enough news to fill its pages. For the November issue at least, this proved to be no problem. Although the missing jewels and the story behind Malcolm Ashby's murder was all over the paper before my magazine went to press, I still counted my report as a scoop because it was the only one that was entirely accurate.

In any case, I didn't really mind the more immediate publicity from the newspapers, because it brought in a huge number of generous offers for the remaining chess sets I was selling on eBay, far more than Steven had paid for them. His association with the famous Milton Keynes jewellery heist, of which the concealed rubies were indeed a part, seemed to add value. Nell Little was right when she said things are worth what people are prepared to pay for them.

I just hope my customers are equally willing to purchase the mountain of knitted stuff Mum's gone home to create. I'm very glad we've already agreed she's going to deliver the first batch when she comes to stay with me for a proper village Christmas, whatever that may be. I'm looking forward to finding out.

In all the excitement, I'd almost forgotten about the ketchup slogan painted on my tea terrace. But in the end, it didn't take a genius – or Mum – to solve that mystery. When I went up to Suki's Stores a couple of weeks later to deliver her copy of the November *Parish News*, I found her in an unusually conciliatory mood.

'You're doing a great job with the parish mag,' she said, not looking at me. 'You know, I didn't think you'd be up to it, but you're doing a much better job than that snoopy old spy who was doing it before you.'

Perhaps she was damning me with faint praise, but I was prepared to take it as a win.

'I thought you were exploiting the village when you started using the mag to shout about your chess sale, expecting everyone to pay a fortune for something they didn't need. But Jack Dauntless was in here earlier telling me how generous you've been to the school, and I'm sorry. I didn't mean to upset you. I should never have done it. So. Sorry. That's all. I didn't really mean no harm.'

To cover her embarrassment, she picked up the charity collection box on the counter, and fiddled with the label, which was starting to peel off the side. It showed a picture of an elephant.

I gasped. 'So, it was you! You're the ketchup messenger!'

She rattled the collection box. 'Yeah, sorry, like I said. It's just that I saw that elephant chess set in your window, and it looked like it was made of ivory. I thought, hurrah, here at last is a cause I can get behind on my own doorstep.' She returned the collection box to its place and leaned on the counter, looking me in the eye. 'Have you seen what those dreadful elephant poachers do?'

Her eyes filled with tears and her bottom lip began to tremble. I never knew she had a vulnerable side. She might make a show of not liking her customers very much, but her concern for suffering animals was clearly genuine.

'There's not usually anything I can do around here to prevent animal cruelty, apart from rattle one of my collection boxes at people when I give them their change, and now so many people pay by card, I can't even do that as often as I used to. I thought this was my chance to make a difference. When I was a little girl at the village school, I thought one day, I'd grow up and work for Dian Fossey's gorillas in Africa, or something like that. But I'm powerless stuck in this shop all day. I can't even take time out to join the village protestors against the hunt. I don't suppose my life will ever be any different.'

With a pang of sadness, I wondered how many young villagers might find it so hard to move away from Little Pride to fulfil their ambitions. Then I had an idea.

'I tell you what, Suki, there are other ways of helping those causes without leaving the village. How would you like to start writing a monthly column drawing attention to animal welfare issues in the *Little Pride Parish News*? It could do with more articles besides local event news and announcements. If you do it well, you'll encourage lots of locals to support your cause, which could be worth much more than the odd pennies in your collection box. These charities need people to spread the word for them just as much as they need workers out in the field. How about that?'

Suki's face lit up. 'Me? Really? You want me to write about saving animals every month?'

I nodded. 'With your obvious passion, I'm sure you could make it interesting.'

'Wow. Yes, of course. I'd love to, Alice, thank you.'

I grinned.

'So,' I said, 'does that mean we're friends again?'

Suki took a step back from the counter. 'Friends? Don't push your luck, mate. I never said I wanted to be your friend.'

But her cheeky grin told me otherwise.

As I strolled back out into the high street, looking forward to my first proper date with Robert that night, a romantic home-cooked meal at his house, all finally seemed right in Little Pride. At least for the time being.

* * *

MORE FROM DEBBIE YOUNG

Another book from Debbie Young, *Driven to Murder*, is available to order now here:

www.mybook.to/DriventoBackAd

ACKNOWLEDGEMENTS

Let me confess here and now that, like Alice, I cannot play chess. My big brother taught me when I was little, I suspect so that he had an opponent he could always beat, and that put me right off. I've always preferred Scrabble, taught to me at an early age by my grandmother. Only in later life did I realise that this highly intelligent lady often played poorly herself in order to let me win.

However, I have always been intrigued by beautiful chess sets, and the Isle of Lewis chessmen featured in this story are my favourite, not least because they always remind me of the delightful children's stories about Noggin the Nog, created by Oliver Postgate and Peter Firmin in 1959 and televised as animations throughout my childhood.

I'm grateful to my husband Gordon Young for explaining any technical details of chess sets that I needed along the way, including his view that serious chess players don't play with novelty pieces.

Thanks also to my daughter Laura for helping with the typing of the first draft, which I always write by hand.

As ever, my publisher Boldwood Books has been wonderfully supportive and encouraging, especially editorial director and mentor Rachel Faulkner-Willcocks, copy editor Becca Allen, and proofreader Emily Reader. Together, they've saved me from myself when I got tangled up in dubious timeframes and tricky plot twists. I know Boldwood's marketing team will do a superb job sending the finished book out into the world and to eager readers everywhere.

Now back to my writing desk, plotting the third Cotswold Curiosity Shop adventure. I can't wait to return to Little Pride!

ABOUT THE AUTHOR

Debbie Young is the much-loved author of the Sophie Sayers and St Brides cosy crime mysteries. She lives in a Cotswold village, where she runs the local literary festival, and has worked at Westonbirt School, both of which provide inspiration for her writing.

Sign up to Debbie Young's mailing list for news, competitions and updates on future books.

Visit Debbie's Website: www.authordebbieyoung.com

Follow Debbie on social media:

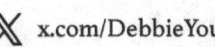 x.com/DebbieYoungBN

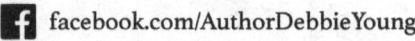 facebook.com/AuthorDebbieYoung

bookbub.com/authors/debbie-young

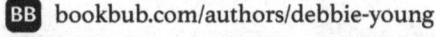 instagram.com/debbieyoungauthor

ALSO BY DEBBIE YOUNG

A Gemma Lamb Cozy Mystery

Dastardly Deeds at St Bride's

Sinister Stranger at St Bride's

Wicked Whispers at St Bride's

Artful Antics at St Bride's

A Sophie Sayers Cozy Mystery

Murder at the Vicarage

Best Murder in Show

Murder in the Manger

Murder at the Well

Springtime for Murder

Murder at the Mill

Murder Lost and Found

Murder in the Highlands

Driven to Murder

The Cotswold Curiosity Shop Mysteries

Death at the Old Curiosity Shop

Death at the Village Chess Club